Emma's
ORPHANS

D0468659

Emma's ORPHANS

LOREE LOUGH

WHITAKER
HOUSE

Publisher's note:
This novel is a work of fiction. References to real events, organizations, or places are used in a fictional context. Any resemblances to actual persons, living or dead, are entirely coincidental.

All Scripture quotations are taken from the King James Version of the Holy Bible.

Emma's Orphans

Loree Lough
www.loreelough.com

IBSN: 978-1-60374-719-6
eBook ISBN: 978-1-60374-720-2
Printed in the United States of America
© 2013 by Loree Lough

Whitaker House
1030 Hunt Valley Circle
New Kensington, PA 15068
www.whitakerhouse.com

Library of Congress Cataloging-in-Publication Data (Pending)

No part of this book may be reproduced or transmitted in any form or by any means, electronic or mechanical—including photocopying, recording, or by any information storage and retrieval system—without permission in writing from the publisher. Please direct your inquiries to permissionseditor@whitakerhouse.com.

1 2 3 4 5 6 7 8 9 10 11 20 19 18 17 16 15 14 13

Emma's Orphans is dedicated to all the men and women who helped parentless children find loving Christian homes between 1853–1929; to Larry for years of enduring my "fiction addiction"; to my daughters for their unwavering support; to my dear friend, author Carolyn Greene for good solid advice; and to Whitaker House editor Courtney Hartzel for her gentle word-guidance.

PROLOGUE

Ellicott City, Maryland
September 1, 1865

Death and dying seemed to dominate her life lately. She'd lost scores of friends in the horrible war between the States that ended just months ago, and now her beloved aunt had joined them. It was not as dramatic a passing as those who'd died in battle; Stella simply went in her sleep. And as the cancer slowly ate away at her, Emma simply devoted herself to caring for the woman who raised her from infancy.

Emma and Jenni Wright walked arm in arm from the cemetery—their first visit to Stella's grave since the funeral—huddled against the unseasonably chilly day. Lost in separate worlds of sadness and grief as they headed for their buggy, neither took much notice of the commotion half a block away.

Jenni looked up at her big sister through tear-clumped lashes. "Do you think Aunt Stella will be lonely in heaven?"

Emma pulled her a bit closer and blinked back hot tears of her own. "No," she said, smiling, "not with all God's angels to keep her company."

Sighing, the girl gave a satisfied nod. "Angels…she'll like that. Mrs. Henderson taught us in Sunday school that the angels make beautiful music, with harps and flutes and—"

The ruckus up the street intensified, and Emma and Jenni jumped onto the wooden walkway, staring wide-eyed as the horses hitched to John Evans' wagon reared up, ears flattened and teeth bared as they cut loose with several trumpeting cries.

The girl huddled closer to her big sister. "What's got them so spooked?" she whimpered, chewing the knuckle of her forefinger. "I don't see anyth…"

The snake, coiled and ready for attack, rattled its deadly warning, freezing the question in her throat. Time seemed to freeze, too, and the next moments passed at a painfully plodding pace.

Grabbing Jenni by the hand, Emma darted into the church. Her boot heels echoed as she ran down the center aisle in search of the pastor, a deacon…anyone who might help the blacksmith regain control of his team.

She stopped at the altar. "Pray for them, Jenni," she whispered huskily. "Ask God to send them help!"

The melee outside punctuated Emma's instructions, and she raced back down the aisle. "Maybe someone has heard the noise by now," she said, half-dragging the terrified girl behind her.

From opposite sides of the street, James Griffen and Walter Turner charged up to the horses, hollering "Whoa!" and "Stop!" as they reached for the harness. But the crazed beasts' rock-hard hooves stomped the ground and clawed the air, preventing them from getting close enough to take hold.

Drawn by the blacksmith's agitated voice, Emma focused on his face. "Are you mad?" John shouted at the men. "Get back! You'll be trampled!" Unconsciously, she winced with him as the reins dug bloody gouges into his bare hands.

John Evans had won the county fair's Muscle Man contest eight years in a row, single-handedly built his house, and the two-storied blacksmith shop behind it as well. But even his formidable strength seemed feeble in comparison to the power of the panic-stricken animals. Their eyes rolled wildly in their twitching, pitching heads as spittle foamed at the corners of their mouths. The wagon lurched and creaked as they tried to sidestep the hissing, slithering snake, tossing the wagon's passengers about like rag dolls.

"Oh, John!" Mrs. Evans shrieked, gripping the seat back as she looked behind her into the wagon bed. "The children..."

The words were no sooner out of her mouth than both front wheels lifted from the ground, teetering in the air for a silent, eerie moment, as if suspended by cables from above.

And then, despite John's attempts to restrain them, the horses bolted, yanking him from his seat. He tumbled forward and quickly disappeared in the thick cloud of dust, as did his screams.

Instinctively, his wife reached out to save him, but in the futile attempt to pull her beloved from the thundering holocaust of hooves, she lost her balance and met the same grisly end.

"Dear God in heaven," Emma whispered. "Help them."

And then, seemingly from out of nowhere, a man dressed all in black rode up beside the runaway team and, crouched low in the saddle, guided his big black steed until he matched the team's furious pace, step for frantic step.

His wide-brimmed hat blew off when he reached out to snag a breast harness, and it zigzagged lazily on the autumn breeze before floating to the ground. With a groan, he leapt onto the nearest horse's back. His mare slowed to a trot as her master was carried away by her terrified cousins, then meandered to the water trough beside the road.

Emma held Jenni tighter still, trembling with helpless fear. Had it really been just two days ago that she'd removed splinters from their boyish hands? Splinters put there by fishing poles they'd fashioned from branches felled in the last thunderstorm?

Ten years before, Matthew Evans had been the first child the inexperienced young nurse had helped bring into the world. Two years and a dozen babies later, Emma delivered Billy on her own. *Lord God Almighty*, she prayed, *let the stranger stop the horses in time to save the boys*. She could only hope there was time enough for her prayer to reach God's ear.

During one tick in time, the wagon hit a rock in the road; in the next, all four wheels left the ground, breaking Billy's death grip on the side rail. As the vehicle crashed back onto solid earth, he was catapulted high in a graceful arc, as though he was taking a frolicking summer leap off Great Rock Gorge to swim in the refreshing waters of the Patapsco River. A small dust cloud puffed up around him when he landed, slowly blanketing him with a powdery veil.

Emma hung her fingertips from her bottom teeth, waiting for him to show any sign of life. But the boy did not cry out in pain or clutch a broken limb in agony: time had stopped for Billy Evans.

In the next millisecond, residents of Ellicott City threw open windows and doors to investigate the violent noise that cracked their peaceful September morning. All eyes zeroed in on the wagon, now a half-mile down the road.

Men, women, and children alike rushed forward as the stranger brought the team to a grinding, grit-spewing halt. He sat for a moment, head hanging and shoulders slumped, as if in prayer, then slid down from the horse's back and quickly secured the glassy-eyed, sweaty team to the hitching post outside the general store.

Without a word, he walked around to the back of the wagon and held up his arms. After one intense moment, Matthew sagged into them.

"Who is he?" Jenni whispered as he headed toward them. "He looks like someone I know."

As he made his way nearer the murmuring crowd, Emma admitted to herself that the girl was right; the stranger *did* look strikingly familiar.

The townsfolk gave him a wide berth as he walked determinedly up to the boardwalk and put the boy into her arms. "Get him inside," he growled. With a jerk of his dark-haired head, he gestured toward the street, where three rumpled bodies lay sprawled in silent, motionless heaps. "He doesn't need to see that."

Emma glanced in the direction he indicated, but the gruesome sight caused her to quickly avert her eyes. Why he chose hers from all the worried faces staring into his, Emma didn't know.

The dark brows dipped low in the center of his forehead. "Well," he grated, "what're you waitin' for? Can't you see he needs tendin'?"

Somehow, Emma sensed his rage was not intended for her, but for the event that ended three lives, for she saw in his near-black eyes compassion and concern for the boy he'd saved.

She focused on Matthew, whose heaving chest and rumpled clothes told of the physical ordeal he'd survived, whose trembling hands and quivering lower lip stated the emotional trauma he'd suffered. She stood him on his feet, then knelt to make herself child-sized. Placing both hands on the boy's shoulders, Emma turned him to face her. Though he made eye contact, Matt seemed unable to see her. *Dear God,* she prayed, *tell me what he needs to hear.*

"Matthew," she began quietly, giving his shoulders a gentle shake. "Matthew?"

As the fog lifted, the boy struggled to stanch the tears that filled his eyes. His voice seemed deeper and far too raspy to belong to one so young. "Are they...are they all...dead?"

"We'll know soon enough," answered the stranger.

Jenni leaned forward to whisper into Emma's ear. "He talks funny, like Mr. O'Neil; I think he must be Irish."

Ignoring Jenni, Matt looked away from Emma to focus on the man's face. "My pa always says you shouldn't sugarcoat the truth. You won't feed me a line of nonsense, will you?" He stiffened his back. "'Cause I ain't no baby, y'know. My pa says men don't cry."

Jabbing a thumb into his chest, he added in a gravelly whisper, "I can handle the truth."

The man was covered in dust from boots to beard, and the palms of his hands were raw and bleeding. If he noticed, he didn't seem to care. Down on one knee, he gently chucked the boy's chin. "Good or bad," he said softly, "you'll get nothin' but the truth from me, son. You've got me word on it."

None of the onlookers had budged since he approached, carrying the hefty lad like a babe in arms. Emma scanned their faces and saw that though they likely didn't recognize him either, they also instinctively believed his word.

Matt nodded and put his hand into Emma's. "I'll be inside," he said as she led him into the bank, "waiting to hear..."

Emma and Jenni, Matt and the stranger seemed oblivious to the mayhem in the street behind them. The doctor stood over Billy's body, somberly shaking his head. The undertaker knelt beside John, frowning. And the town barber crouched beside Martha, hiding his face behind one hand.

As the man in black headed for his horse, someone hollered out, "You saved that boy's life. You're a hero, man!"

He scowled into the crowd. "Hero?" he snarled. "Didn't save the brother."

Grimacing, he climbed into his saddle and drove the horse hard toward the Patapsco.

ONE

February 1, 1866

I've decided to change my name to Matt Evans Wright."

The boy made the announcement over supper, six months to the day after burying his entire family. He popped the last of his biscuit into his mouth and washed it down with a generous gulp of milk. Breathing a whispered "Ahhh," he drew his sleeve across his mouth. "Ma and Pa and Billy would have wanted it this way, I'm sure of it." And then he smiled calmly, awaiting Emma's response.

But she had no idea how to respond. As she looked into his clear blue eyes, her heart ached with love for him. Someday, she knew, he'd become a fine, strong man, and the proof of that was the stoic way he reserved his grieving for the deepest, darkest hours of the night. Last night, when his tormented moans awakened her, she hurried into his room and pulled him into her arms. "There, there," she'd cooed, running her fingers through soft blond curls. "It's all right, sweet boy; it was only a bad dream. You're all right now. Emma's here."

When at last he roused from the nightmare, and realized where he was, Matt had scrambled sleepily into her lap and tucked his face into the crook of her neck. In the bright light of day, he would never have clung to her that way. Emma smiled fondly, remembering the way he wrinkled his face and held up his hands in mock defensiveness each time her motherly instincts compelled her to reach out as he passed, to lovingly muss his hair, or press a kiss to his cheek.

As his tears abated, a smile curved his lips. It seemed a peaceful smile, Emma thought, but how peaceful could it really be for this brave boy who'd lost everything and everyone in two quick ticks of the clock? "Peaceful enough to fall asleep," she whispered gently, tucking the covers under his chin and kissing his cheek before tiptoeing from his room.

"Well," he said now, tucking in one corner of his mouth, "what do you think? Matt Evans Wright. Isn't it a fine, strong name?"

His question snapped Emma back to the present. Her heart swelled with growing love for this rough-and-tumble boy, for his question was proof positive that he thought of her as his substitute mother...already! Much as she'd love to keep him with her forever, it would be cruel to give him false hope. She already begun the process of finding a proper home for him, with a mother and a father and...

In a more serious tone, she said, "Yes, it's a fine, strong name, but let's see what Judge Thompson says before you start writing it at the top of your school papers."

Matt's nose crinkled as though he inhaled the telltale scent of a skunk. "Why does that old buzzard have any say in it?" He jabbed a thumb into his chest. "I'm the one oughta be decidin' where I'll live, and who I'll live with."

In a perfect world, Emma would have gently corrected his grammar. But theirs was far from a perfect world. She took a deep breath and laid her fork beside her plate.

"In a perfect world," Emma cautioned, "children would have complete control over such things." She shook her head sadly. "I'm afraid we don't live in a perfect world."

Matt pointed at Jenni, who sat quietly at the other end of the table. "Then, how come that ol' judge let her live here when her mother died?"

Jenni shoved her plate forward and folded her hands primly on the table, then pursed her lips. "For your information," she began, "Judge Thompson didn't decide, because he wasn't around when my mama died."

"Then who decided?" he demanded, his voice rising in pitch and volume. "'Cause that's the fella I want to see!" As if hearing his own distress, Matt took a deep breath and looked at Emma. "I want to live here," he said softly, calmly. "You're a good mother. What more should matter to that old—"

"Now, now," Emma interrupted, smiling slightly. "Judge Thompson isn't an old—"

"He's a mean old grouch," Jenni chimed in. "I've never seen him talk to children except to scold them. I'll bet he doesn't even like children. He's the last person who ought to be deciding things that will affect them for the rest of their lives!"

The boy raised both brows and nodded gratefully. When he looked at Emma again, fear glinted in his pale blue eyes and his lower lip quivered a bit. "I want to stay with you," he whispered hoarsely. "I want to stay here."

Before the accident, Matt had been a rowdy, hardy boy, who thought nothing of climbing to the top of the tallest oak, or balancing precariously like a tightrope walker on the fallen tree that connected Great Rock Gorge to Swan Point. She never saw him cry, not even the time when he was four, when he fell halfway down the stairs in the choir loft and broke his arm.

Since losing his family, he hadn't been so inclined to take little-boy chances with his safety. Oh, he made a great show of puffing up his chest and poking out his chin with male bravado when his pals were within earshot. But he also made sure to keep Emma within his sights.

Narrowing one eye, he crossed both arms over his chest. "How much pull do you have?"

"Pull?" Emma giggled. "I'm afraid I don't understand."

"How much weight is in your word? How important is what you say to the people of this town?"

He sounded so much like his father! Many times, she heard John Evans ask similar questions at town hall meetings, or as the men gathered in the feed and grain, discussing politics. Matt needed a man's influence, as evidenced by this attempt to emulate his pa. Would it be in his best interests to intervene on the boy's behalf, and insist that he remain in her care? Or would Matt be better off in a home led by a strong Christian male?

"I heard them talking in town the other day," Jenni was saying.

"You heard who talking?" Emma wanted to know.

The girl shrugged. With a slight nod of her head, she said, "Oh, just a bunch of old hens."

"Jenni!" Emma scolded. "Is that any way to talk?"

Blushing, she swallowed. "Well, that's what Mr. O'Neil called them, right to their faces," the girl said in her own defense.

Emma frowned and shook a finger at the children. "Mr. O'Neil needs to exercise a little restraint. Just because he's an old man doesn't mean he can go around saying whatever pops into his thick Irish skull!"

Matt and Jenni hid childish giggles behind their hands, inspiring Emma to cross both arms over her chest as she silently admitted that in taking them to task, she had spoken ill of O'Neil!

"All right, you two," she said, lifting one brow.

"Don't you want to hear what the old..." Matt snickered, then wiggled in his chair to assume a more serious posture..."what the dear ladies were talking about?"

If the truth be told, she thought, doing her best to hide a grin, *the good ladies of Ellicott City can sound like a bunch of old hens when they get together for one of their gossip-fests!* She feigned a bored expression; it was just as true that she was curious. "Out with it, then. What did they say?"

"They said no one would object to you taking care of me, because I'm a girl and you're a girl." Jenni glanced at Matt. Then, eyes on Emma once more, she continued. "But Matt is a boy, and he needs a man's firm hand, they said."

"A man's firm hand?" Matt repeated. "What does that mean?"

"Someone who'll wallop you a good one when you get out of line," Jenni explained.

He gasped, then licked his lips. "But...but..." His eyes misted as his lips formed a tight line. "I didn't mind it when my pa walloped me," he said, shaking a fist in the air, "'cause he always said he was doin' it for my own good. But nobody else better try, or I'll wallop 'em right back!"

"Oh, as if you could stand up to a man twice your size," Jenni pointed out, rolling her eyes.

"I could if I had to!" he persisted, stubbornly blinking back the tears that welled in his eyes.

Emma hurried to his side and, while kneeling on the ground, wrapped her arms around him. "Matthew," she began, "no one is going to wallop you if I have anything to say about it."

He studied her face. "You mean it?"

Standing, she assumed a boxer's stance, crouching and balling her own hands into fists. "I mean it!"

A tiny giggle bubbled from Jenni's lips, and she clamped her hands over her mouth to silence it. Grinning, Matt met the girl's eyes. "Remind me to be on my best behavior around here, 'cause if she did take a mind to wallop me, I might end up in Carroll County!"

∽

Emma paced the floor that night, in deep concentration as she tried to figure out what she might do to ensure Matt could remain in her care. Her heart beat double-time and her pulse raced. She hadn't been this upset since that letter came...the one delivered in person by Horace Talbott, barely a week after her aunt's death. She slipped into her room, and opened the tiny cedar chest that held her few pieces of jewelry and the letter. She brought it into the parlor and sat in the big wooden rocker near the hearth. Splaying the pages across her lap, she remembered...

She had risen earlier than usual that morning, and was taking a batch of biscuits from the oven when Horace rapped at her back door. He was the only man in town who'd invited her to a church picnic, or a holiday party—or anything else for that matter—in two years. It didn't seem to matter one whit to him that she towered over him the way an adult towers over a child, or that she likely outweighed him by fifty pounds. It was getting harder and harder to find polite ways to turn him down, and she hoped he hadn't come to ask her to accompany him to the Valentine's Day social; had she been out of bed long enough for her brain to come up with another kindly reason to say "No"?

"What brings you out so early?" she asked, opening the door wide to admit him.

But Horace had stood on the tiny porch, touched a finger to the brim of his black derby and said, "I'm afraid this is not a social call, Emma." He lifted his pointy chin and held out an official-looking envelope. "Your aunt asked that I..."

The sharp knob of his Adam's apple bobbed up and down as he ran a bony finger under the starched collar of his white shirt. "She asked that I deliver this to you upon her death." Pulling a red bandana from the inside pocket of his suit coat, he blotted perspiration from his furrowed brow and sighed. "I'm terribly sorry," he said, waving the envelope under her nose, "but I've had it in my wall safe so long, I forgot all about it until last evening. I found it while—"

"What's in it?" Emma interrupted.

"I'm afraid I have no idea."

"But...but you were Aunt Stella's attorney. Surely...."

He held up a hand to silence her. "She only asked me to hold onto it for her. Nothing more."

Emma gave him a suspicious, sideways glance. "I don't believe you for a minute, Horace. You didn't earn the nickname 'Lion Pants' because you don't take well to bad news, yet look at you, sweating like a pig, and on this thirty-degree morning no less!" She tucked in one corner of her mouth to add, "I don't mind telling you, I'm not looking forward to reading any message that's had such an effect on the likes of you!"

He removed his hat, and, holding it by the brim, tapped it against his thigh. "You're probably right to suspect there's bad news in here," he said, holding out the envelope. "Stella was greatly distressed the day she brought it to my office. Her face was all puffy and her eyes were red from crying, and it was all she could do to get the request out without starting up the waterworks again."

Horace looked away then, and focused for a moment on some unknown spot across the room. When he met her eyes again, it was to say, "She was so upset that I never asked about its contents. I simply agreed to keep it in my safe until her death, nothing more."

Emma took the letter, trembling.

"If you...if you...need to talk," he stammered as he headed down the walk, "or need any advice...you know where to find me."

"Thank you, Horace."

"Just doing my job," he said, climbing into his buggy.

But Emma knew better. Horace Talbott was the county's most prominent attorney. He could easily have paid a messenger to deliver the letter. She opened her mouth to say so, but he was gone before the first words formed on her tongue.

She closed the door quietly, then crossed to the table and thanked the Lord she had already filled her mug with steaming coffee, because her hands were shaking so badly, she'd have burned herself if she'd poured a cup at that point.

On the envelope, Aunt Stella had written "Emma Wright."

A glance at the clock told Emma that Jenni would awaken soon. If the letter contained bad news—and everything in her told her that it did—she'd best get the matter dealt with now, so she'd have time to get her emotions under control before the child woke up.

Emma slumped onto a nearby stool and broke the envelope's seal. Taking a sip of coffee, she removed the crisp pages and read:

June 2, 1860

My dear, dear Emma,

We have suspected for some time now that these pains in my stomach were caused by more than cabbage and beans, and now that we know it's the cancer, I feel obliged to set a few things straight before the end comes. Doctor Farley says it could be years, but I will not take the chance; it might only be months. It seems right and just that I'm setting the record straight on your birthday, the day my lies began.

My life is complete for having loved you, for having been loved by you. You were a beautiful child, sweet Emma, with a beautiful soul, who trustingly put yourself in my care. You never demanded to know how it came to be that you were being raised by a maiden aunt, and for that I will be eternally grateful. But now, you have a right to know everything, everything I had no right to keep from you. The time has come, as they say, to come clean.

As you know, I was raised on a farm in Lancaster, Pennsylvania—Amish country, through and through. The simple life was good enough for me, and I lived it without complaint until my sixteenth birthday. I went into town that day, as I always did on Tuesday to deliver eggs for my mother, and there I met the most handsome young man I'd ever seen. His name was Emmit Wright.

He had all the things to turn a young girl's head. He was a life-loving twenty-one-year-old man with sparkling blue eyes and honey-blond hair. That wide, easy smile seemed painted on his face, and he had the voice of an archangel. But mostly, Emma, he had such a big heart! I could talk to Emmit about anything, and he to me. We shared our hopes and dreams and fears… and we fell in love. On one Tuesday, it seemed, we were talking innocently; the next, we were holding hands, and before I knew it, he completely surrounded me with the warmth of his love.

And then all that was bright in my world turned dark, for I learned that I was going to have Emmit's baby. The family was angry with me for committing the sin of fornication. I knew that I had sinned, yet I was deeply hurt by their response. After many long and serious meetings with the church elders, my penance was decided: I would be shunned.

They sent me by stagecoach to York, where I would stay with Doctor Zachary Josephs and his wife Jane. They had no children of their own, and cared for me as if I was their own. Not a word of recrimination was spoken regarding my condition. They seemed to understand (though I never told them) that I grieved not only for the family I had been cast out of but for the young man I loved too much. The only proof I have that they understood these things was the gentle looks they gave me each time I came from my room, eyes red and puffy from crying over my losses.

When at last you were born, they fussed and cooed like real grandparents. I called you Em and I think the Josephs knew why: so that each time I spoke your name, I would be reminded of my one true love.

I'm told Emmit searched nearly two years for me. It did my heart good knowing that he loved me that much. I have sent prayers heavenward every day since then, hoping he found peace and contentment in his life, wherever he chose to live it.

You were only three when we moved to Maryland, dear Emma. I had abused the good doctor's kindness far too long as it was. I overheard him telling his wife about an old friend, who'd written about a clinic he would open in Ellicott City. I pleaded with the doctor to write the friend on my behalf: Mrs. Josephs was a nurse, too, you see, and had trained me well. I convinced them it would be a fresh new start for you and me, and he sent a letter of introduction ahead.

We rode our first train to Baltimore, and Doctor Aubrey Farley met us there. Oh, but he was a grim-faced, straight-backed man! I don't think I've ever been more frightened than I was that day when he greeted us at the station. He never smiled, not even with his eyes. As he talked from the city to our new home, it became apparent that Dr. Josephs, knowing his rigid and judgmental personality, had stretched the truth about me a bit in his letter.

Dr. Farley was of a mind that I was a maiden aunt who'd taken in an orphaned niece. I could see right off that to tell the truth was a surefire way to end up alone and unemployed in a strange city. I had no money to get back to York, and couldn't impose further on the Josephs, who had already been so kind to me.

And so I decided on the buggy ride between Baltimore and the new clinic that while I wouldn't further deceive Dr. Farley, I wouldn't offer the truth until I'd earned enough money to set up housekeeping in another city.

Sadly, sweet Emma, that day never came. There always seemed to be some reason why Dr. Farley couldn't pay my full salary. Either the medicines for the clinic cost more than he expected, or equipment to furnish it was more expensive than anticipated. Things routinely broke down and fell apart, had to be repaired or replaced. And how could I complain when he explained his reasons for not paying me; he was providing us with clean lodgings, three meals a day, and a young girl (who also lived in their house) to care for you while I worked.

It took years to save enough money to get an apartment of our own. And just when it was looking like we could hold our heads above water, there was one more expense: Jenni came along.

You never asked a single question when I brought her home. Not "Where did she come from?" or "Why is she here?" You simply sat on the sofa and opened your arms wide. "Can I hold her?" you asked. When I laid her on your lap, your eyes filled with tears. "She's beautiful, Aunt Stella," you said. "Like one of the cherubs in the stained glass windows at church... only prettier." And from that day on, you opened wide your heart, and shared what little you had with Jenni. It is you who are the angel, my sweet Emma. So now you shall know the answers to questions you never asked:

I was alone in the clinic that morning when the constable brought Jenni's mother to me. She was young—perhaps fifteen or sixteen—and dressed like a beggar. The officer found her in the train station, alone, with no ticket and not a penny in her pockets. I sat with her for hours, patting her hand and pressing cool cloths to her forehead as she talked about nothing in particular...and I talked about you. No matter what words of comfort I spoke, she would not tell me where she came from or who her family was. To tell, she explained, would be to shame them, for her parents were good Christian people who did not deserve a daughter who committed the terrible sin of fornication. That dreadful word again! My heart went out to her, of course, for I understood exactly how she felt.

Jenni's mother was not a healthy girl, as I was when I learned you were on the way, nor was she blessed with a loving couple to care for her as the baby grew within her. I don't imagine she ate well during her long months on the road, and likely hadn't rested much, either. Her weariness showed in the hollows beneath her blue eyes.

The baby came after many hours of hard, agonizing labor. Afterward, some members of the church said her pain was her well-deserved penance for sin. I will not presume to know the mind of God, but I'm certain she had not done anything in her short life to deserve what came next.

The poor child began to hemorrhage, and nothing I did stanched the flow of her life's blood. Sensing the end was near, she whispered into my ear, "Call her Jenni, not Jennifer" she said, "just Jenni." It was her own name, you see. "When you call her Jenni, it will be as if a part of me lives on."

She took for granted I would keep her baby. I suggested the child might be better off with a loving couple who could give her far more than me, an unmarried woman raising a child alone. "You love your Emma," she whispered. "I see it in your eyes and hear it in your voice. I want my Jenni to grow up with love like that." She was dying, and we both knew it. How could I have refused her?

So now you know the truth, my dear Emma. The whole truth, and nothing but, as they say in the courtroom. For as long as I can remember, I have gone to bed each night with a pain in my stomach for keeping the truth from you. Perhaps God will ease the pain of my sickness now that I have, at long last, unburdened myself. They say confession is good for the soul; I say it does nothing but burden the listener.

Oh, dear Emma, I pray you can find it in your heart to forgive me for not having told you everything sooner. I've lived the lie so long; I didn't know how to set it right. I have no courage, I've discovered, and it was my weakness that kept me quiet. I feared that if I told you, and saw disappointment in your eyes, it would have killed me.

I know in my heart you will continue to take care of little Jenni, just as you've always taken care of her. Yes, my life has been complete for having loved and been loved by you. You, however, deserved a better mother than I could ever have been. Still, you did well with what God handed you. Just look at how you've turned out! I love you now, and when I am gone, I will love you still. I am proud, so very proud, to have been,

Your mother

Dabbing at her damp eyes with the corner of a lacy handkerchief, Emma leaned back in the rocker and sighed. She read the letter a hundred times already, and understood only too well why Stella believed it necessary to keep the truth from the Farleys. They were, as Stella described, a grim, judgmental pair. But even if she read the letter a hundred times more, Emma didn't think she'd ever understand why Stella felt the need to deceive her.

She lived her whole life with the woman. They laughed and cried together, worked and relaxed together, prayed and planned together. How could she have spent twenty-six years under the same roof with Aunt Stella, and not have known her at all! It shook Emma's world to learn that she was so deeply and deliberately deceived by the one person she trusted the most.

Admittedly, some good things came from those years—Jenni, for one. There was no denying Emma loved the child who'd been raised as her little sister. They resembled one another enough to have been born of the same parents, with their gleaming blond hair and glittering blue eyes, pale freckled skin and tall willowy builds. Indeed, if Emma married at fifteen, she might have had a daughter who looked just like Jenni.

Before the letter arrived, Emma believed herself to have been orphaned at birth. But each time she read it, she was forced to admit that, like Matt, she, too, had recently been left alone in a world filled with families.

Lips taut in grim determination, Emma resolved to do every-thing in her power to keep Matt with her. They were two of a kind. Soul mates, sharing a recent aloneness. He needed her love and guidance, protection and care. Who could understand him better than the woman who had experienced his pain...twice!

"I've decided to change my name to Matt Evans Wright; a fine strong name, don't you think?" he'd said at supper. "Matthew Evans Wright," Emma whispered. After rolling it over and over on her tongue, she smiled at the sound of it. *It is a fine strong name, and I want it to be his name.*

She had no idea how, but she would make it happen. And she'd begin the process first thing in the morning.

⁓

While Jenni was off spending the day at her best friend Carolyn's house, Emma brought Matt with her to the bank. It was time, at last, to do as her aunt—her mother—had instructed in the will, and put Emma's name on the woman's account.

Matt, bored after the first five minutes of waiting as Emma discussed the matter with the bank manager, asked the woman behind the counter for a pencil and a piece of paper. Madeline Campbell handed him two sheets of fancy bank stationery and a matching envelope. She leaned over the counter and looked both ways, then narrowed her eyes and spoke in low tones.

"Be careful not to make a mess," she warned, waving the pen like a wand, "when you dip this into the inkwell."

Matt smiled up at the pretty young teller. "Thank you, ma'am," he said softly. "I'll be careful, I promise."

He tiptoed across the marble-floored space and chose the counter farthest from where Emma and Mr. Prentice sat talking. The surreptitious mood created by the teller's conspiratorial whis-pers enveloped Matt. Hunched over the table, hiding the pages between his arms, he touched the point of the pen to the ink.

To: Lee
From: Pickett

Squinting with concentration as he considered what to write next, Matt watched a spider climb up the plaster wall and disappear behind the huge oil portrait of the bank's founder.

Sir,

> *We have succeeded in fooling the Union army! The foolish northerners think they have won the war! Ha, ha, ha, the last laugh will be ours!*

Matt glanced at the grandfather clock near the double entry doors and took note of the time: ten thirty-six.

> *Our spies have informed us that the Yankees have a huge savings account at First Bank and Trust on Main Street in Ellicott City. If we blow up the bank, they will not have enough money to buy cannonballs for their cannons or shot for their muskets! So we will attack at precisely ten forty-five. If any of your men are in the First Bank and Trust building, get them out of there quick or they will be blown to smithereens when we aim our big guns at the bank!*

> *Very truly yours,*
> *Mr. George Pickett*

"Oops!" he whispered, drawing a neat line through "Mr." and writing "General" above it. Grinning mischievously, Matt blotted the page, folded it in thirds, and slid it into the matching envelope. "Top Secret!" he wrote in big bold letters across its front. "Do not read unless you are General Robert E. Lee!"

He walked to where two elegant divans faced one another on opposite sides of a gleaming cherry wood table, and stuffed the envelope between two cushions, making sure one corner of it stood out conspicuously from the green leather upholstery. Hand over his grinning mouth, Matt dashed back to the wall, where he pretended to be engrossed in reading the newspaper he'd found folded on the counter, and waited to see the response his message would get.

Three grown-ups passed the sofa before one took note of the envelope. The bespectacled chap slowed his steps as he raised a curious brow. Then, frowning, he resumed his pace and didn't stop walking until he stood at the teller's window.

The heavy wooden doors squeaked as another customer entered the bank. Matt's heart lurched when he saw who it was. It had been six months since he saw him last.

He'd been garbed in black when he so gently lifted Matt from the wagon bed. Today, he wore blue trousers and a collarless white shirt under a black jacket. He'd lost his hat that day; evidently, he'd found it. Almost as if he read Matt's mind, the man whipped it from his head. In the boy's eyes, the man who risked his own life to save him stood taller and broader, even, than his pa.

Though the beard was just as black and the hair a bit longer, his eyes seemed darker and his mouth set tighter. Matt wished he'd smile again, the way he smiled when he'd said, "You'll get nothin' but the truth from me, son; you've got me word on it."

That day, the stranger went into the street where his parents and brother laid dead, and stood, head bowed as in prayer for so long that Matt wondered if he forgot his promise to deliver the truth. But when he turned and faced Matt, the bank's wavy windowpane gave their eye contact an eerie, dizzying effect, like the mirrors in a carnival fun house. But there was hardly a carnival countenance on the man's careworn face. In the minute or so it took him to cross to the boardwalk, Matt almost wished he never demanded to hear the truth.

Emma hadn't left his side, not for an instant. Matt could almost feel her hands now, squeezing his shoulders as if to remind him she was there, right there.

"The news ain't good, son." The man's soft, gravelly voice had washed over Matt like an ocean wave. "I'm afraid...they're gone."

He remembered how it galled him the way his lower lip refused to stop trembling. He wanted to appear strong—manly—as much in control of his emotions as this handsome hero seemed to be. "Gone?" he'd asked.

The dark brows drew together, and for a moment, he averted his gaze. When he looked into Matt's face again, he said one word, a word the boy knew would echo in his head 'til his dying day: "Yes."

The dark brows were drawn together now, too, as though the stranger might be wondering why the boy on the other side of the bank was studying him so intensely. *Does he remember me?* Matt wondered as his ears and cheeks grew hot. Several of the newspaper's pages slipped from his fidgeting fingers and fluttered to the floor, and when he bent to pick them up, he thumped his noggin on the table leg. "Ow," he whispered, wincing as he pressed a palm to his forehead.

He looked up in time to see the man pull the message from between the sofa cushions. Gasping, Matt did the only thing he could think to do, and darted to the desk where Emma and Mr. Prentice sat talking.

"Matthew," Emma said, smiling and patting his hand, "we'll be finished in just a minute. Be a good boy and wait for me on the sofa over there, won't you?"

His eyes darted from Emma's gentle face to the stranger's, and back again. "But...but I..."

She laid a hand on his forearm. "I've a penny in my pocket," she whispered. "It's yours if you do as I ask."

"I'm so sorry for the interruption," he heard Emma say to the manager.

The manager chuckled. "Think nothing of it. The child has been through a lot. Does my heart good to see a smile on his face for a change. Besides," he added, "boys will be boys."

See him smile for a change? Matt repeated to himself, tucking in one corner of his mouth in disgust. *Why, I smile plenty!* With a huff of breath, he crossed both arms over his chest. *That man will obviously say anything to keep a customer happy.*

Indeed, Matt had been working hard to act every bit the carefree boy God intended him to be. How else was he going to keep the nightmares from haunting him during the daytime, too?

The man stood a few yards away, reading Matt's letter. After a moment, he glanced at the clock, then straightened his back. "Ladies and gentlemen," he said in a loud, clear voice, "there's somethin' I think you should know."

TWO

Emma, Prentice, the bank teller, and the bespectacled gent at her window faced him, awaiting the announcement that was important enough to interrupt their business.

Gasping, Matt leapt up. "It was just supposed to be a joke, mister," he said in a grating whisper.

But the joke, Matt realized, was on him, and the proof was the smile shining in the man's dark eyes. "A joke, you say?"

Sighing, Matt could only shake his head.

The bank patrons continued to wait for an explanation for the fellow's outburst. "The time," he said, winking at Matt and satisfying their curiosity at the same time, "is ten forty-five."

There was a moment of stunned silence. "Well, I never," the fussy, bespectacled man complained to Madeline, who tried to hide her grin.

"I'll never understand what gets into some people," Prentice told Emma. "All that fuss to announce the time?"

Emma turned in her seat to focus on Matt. Tilting her head slightly, she raised one brow, her expression communicating what her lips never said: "What did you have to do with that, young man?" He grinned sheepishly and bobbed his head, shuffling from one foot to the other. *I guess you can kiss that penny good-bye*, he said to himself.

As if she read his mind, Emma reached into her pocket and withdrew the coin, dropped it into her purse, and snapped it shut with a finality that answered the boy's unasked question.

"Penny for your thoughts," said the stranger.

Matt couldn't believe his ears. *I'm surrounded by mind readers!* he thought. Sighing with resignation, he slumped onto the green leather sofa. Resting his elbow on its wide, rolled arm, he hid behind his hand while Emma and the stranger made eye contact.

She'd only seen him once—on that awful day when Matt's family was killed. Then, though he was gritty and dusty from his lifesaving ride, Emma didn't think she'd ever seen a more attractive man. Now, in his bright white shirt, he looked even more handsome.

Beards and long hair, in her opinion, made a man look unkempt and dirty. But no such thought crossed her mind looking at the gleaming, neatly trimmed strands surrounding this man's powerful face.

He had broad shoulders, a barrel chest, thick forearms, and big hands...everything that would turn a woman's head. But there was something about those brown eyes that plucked a chord of recognition in her heart. Something had been haunting him for a long, long time, she suspected. Had he, too, lost a loved one—a wife, a child, a parent?

"Miss Wright," the bank manager said, waking her from her reverie, "if you'll just sign right here."

"Of course," she said, turning quickly to accept the pen Prentice offered. As she scraped its nib across the page, Emma wondered how long she'd been staring at the handsome stranger. One look at Prentice provided her answer: long enough for him to send an approving wink across the desk.

Emma sighed inwardly and slid the form toward him, then laid the pen beside it. "How long will it take," she asked, hands folded in her lap, "to move the funds from my...from Aunt Stella's account to mine?" Ever since she'd read that letter, Emma felt foolish referring to Stella as her aunt. But what was she to do? It was what the whole town believed. They also believed Stella had been a devout Christian, honest through and through. Only Emma knew the truth, but what good would come from ruining the woman's reputation?

Prentice stood and smiled patronizingly. "Moving the money will take barely any time at all. You were given power of attorney over your aunt's finances long ago, so everything is in order. Just wait right here, and once I've filed this paperwork, I'll take care of your withdrawal."

Emma walked with calm deliberation to where Matt sat, one hand over his face. "What's gotten into you today?" she asked, perching on the arm of the sofa.

Matt peeked out from between his fingers and squinted one eye. "Sorry, Emma. I don't know."

"I'm sure the boy meant no harm, ma'am."

Startled by the masculine voice so near to her ear, Emma quickly got to her feet, skirts whirling around her ankles as she turned to face him. He stood no more than two feet from her, close enough to see that the sad, soulful eyes were fringed by thick, long lashes. She held out her hand. "I...I'm afraid I never had a chance to thank you properly that day," she began, "for sav—"

He shook his head and held up a silencing hand. "No thanks required, ma'am."

Smiling, she rolled her eyes. "Ma'am? Please! You make me feel like a dotty old woman. The name is Emma," she said. "Emma Wright."

He wrapped his hand around hers and gave it one hearty shake. "And I'm O'Neil," he said, releasing her. "Nate O'Neil."

"Nate," she repeated, her voice a respectful whisper. "What a fine, strong name."

"'Twas me da's name."

"Are you related to Gus O'Neil?"

"Aye. Gus is me da."

Emma nodded. *So that's why he looked so familiar that day; he's the spitting image of his father.*

"We've had many a lively conversation, old Gus and I, about how he snuck his family into the bowels of a coffin ship during the Starving Time."

Chuckling, Nate looked toward the ceiling. "Aye. 'Twas back in '49. And I'd be surprised if he told you the story any fewer than ten times." His smile faded a bit by the time he met her eyes again. "Don't get me wrong...I've nothin' but respect for me da. 'Twas a courageous thing he did, to be sure. I was thirteen at the time, and thought he hung the moon." He gave a nod of his head. "Still do."

"I worked with your mother and sister on a quilt last year. We sold it to raise money for a new pipe organ at the church. They're quite the talented seamstresses."

"Aye. There isn't much me ma doesn't do well, and she taught Suisan everything she knows."

"And your brother! Why, sometimes still I marvel at the clock tower he erected near Oella." She paused, inclining her head. "You have a lovely family, Mr. O'Neil."

"Please, call me Nate."

Emma felt the heat of a blush in her cheeks as he said "And thank you for the kind words about me family."

They stood in awkward silence for a moment until Prentice rescued them. "Miss Wright," he called, "would you be so kind as to step up to the window for a moment?"

Emma made a move to leave, but then thought better of it. "You must let me do something to thank you for saving Matthew—perhaps dinner after services on Sunday?" Winking, she leaned forward slightly and whispered, "I'm told I bake a fine berry pie."

"As I said, thanks aren't necessary." His smile widened. "But berry just happens to be my favorite kind of pie."

A tiny thrill shot through her veins as her heart hammered happily. "Then we'll see you at noon." She started for the teller's window, but stopped halfway there. "Oh, my house is—"

"I know where it is."

Frowning slightly, she tilted her head. "You do? But…"

He was glad for his thick beard; perhaps it hid the flush that crept into his cheeks.

Nate opened his mouth to explain how he knew where she lived when Prentice said, "Oh, Miss Wright…?"

Bless your soul twice, Prentice, Nate thought. He jammed the big hat atop his head and aimed for the doors.

"See you Sunday, then," Emma said, walking backwards toward the teller's window.

"Aye," he said over his shoulder, "noon, straight up."

It wasn't until he stood on the boardwalk that Nate realized he hadn't made his deposit. He couldn't very well go back inside now and have her think he was the town simpleton. He'd just have to wait until she'd finished her business to take care of his own.

Pocketing both hands, he ducked for warmth into the collar of his coat, and headed for the river. He did some of his best thinking on the banks of the Patapsco.

And he had plenty to think about this morning.

Whatever was in your mind, man, to make you agree to have a meal with her? He hadn't been alone with a woman since Laura. "Keep the ring," he'd told his lovely, dark-haired fiancée when he broke off the engagement, "it's the least you deserve."

Nothing could have been further from the truth. In his opinion, no woman deserved to be linked for life to the likes of him—especially not a woman like Laura!

And not a woman like Emma, who by her mere presence had his thoughts turning to wife and family. A decent, marriageable female had every right to expect her man would protect her from harm, care for her always, and love her more than life itself. How could a man like him keep his woman from harm—a man who'd let his comrades down?

Nate climbed onto the stone viaduct built in '35 and surveyed the rushing river waters below. In past think-sessions, he'd walked the entire seven-hundred-foot length of the bridge, inspecting each of the eight elliptical arches that stood sixty feet wide and sixty feet high. He felt small and insignificant in the bridge's shadow. Now, perched on the stone memorial created by John McCartney to honor his crew, he felt nonexistent, for no one would ever erect a monument in his honor!

And if Emma Wright knew what a vile and disgusting secret lurked in his past, he believed, she wouldn't pass the time of day with him, let alone bake him a berry pie.

❦

"They like worms all right," Matt said, "but they like cheese better."

"I don't believe it."

Without taking his eyes from the tip of his fishing pole, Matt shrugged one shoulder. "See for yourself. There's a chunk in my creel, there."

His new friend lifted the lid of the wedge-shaped basket and slipped a hand inside, avoiding the trout that lay on the bottom.

"Tie it to your line good and tight," Matt instructed, "then drop it in the water real slow. Give your pole a little jerk now and then. Makes the cheese bobble in the water like a smaller fish, see, and—"

"I know how to catch a fish," the boy snapped, slamming the creel's lid.

Matt met his companion's eyes. "Could've fooled me," he said haughtily, his voice a coarse whisper.

"I bet I caught my first fish before you caught yours!"

Matt shook his head. "I don't think so, 'cause if you fished ever before in your life, you'd know that to catch anything, you have to be quiet!"

But the boy seemed too busy staring at the moist nugget between his thumb and forefinger to have heard a word Matt said.

"If you eat the bait," Matt pointed out when his fishing buddy licked his lips, "how will you ever find out if cheese catches fish better than worms?"

He only continued to stare at the cheese.

"Didn't you eat breakfast this morning?"

"Ain't had a meal in two days." He met Matt's eyes to add, "Why else would I be sittin' here with the likes of you, tryin' to catch a fish. I don't even like fish, but I'm so hungry, I'd eat a rock if you put a little salt on it."

Matt frowned. He hadn't asked him any questions, not when the boy sauntered out of the woods, not when he sat down beside him. For one thing, Matt rather enjoyed the company. For another, he hadn't been the least bit curious who the boy was, or where he'd came from.

Well, he was curious now.

"Why haven't you eaten in two days? Is your ma too sick to cook or something?"

"My ma is dead," he said matter-of-factly. "So's my pa. The preacher in Richmond sent me here to meet up with a doctor by the name of Farley. He was to deliver me to a family up in the Maryland mountains. But when I got off the train, I saw him standin' on the platform, holdin' up a sign that said 'Curtis Wills.' Took one look at him and said to myself, 'No siree, Curtis; you ain't goin' nowhere near that sour-faced old coot!'" To Matt he said, "If the family he was to hook me up with is even half as mean as he looks, hard to tell what might become of the likes of a colored boy like me. Birds of a feather flock together, y'know."

Matt's frown intensified and his eyes narrowed with suspicion. "Doc Farley was to connect you up with a family, you say? When did he get into the adoption business?"

The boy shrugged. "Dunno. All's I know is he scares me."

Matt nodded. "He scares everybody...you know, my folks are dead, too."

Curtis sat cross-legged beside Matt and began to tie the cheese to his fishing line. "How long?"

"Six months now."

Curtis nodded, too. "Been nearly a year for me. Lost 'em in the war. If I hadn't ducked under the porch, I'd-a-been shot right with 'em." He paused, sighed. "How'd you end up alone?"

"My pa had been in Elk Ridge, diggin' ore. He was a black-smith, y'see, and needed the ore for smelting into pig iron. It's pretty rocky in places, and near as I can tell, a rattler must have climbed into the back of his wagon. Anyways, when Pa stopped to unload, it musta crawled out and scared the horses." He swallowed and took a deep breath. "They reared up and spilled 'em right out of the wagon. My little brother, too. They were..." Matt swallowed. "They were trampled."

"You saw it?"

"Uh-huh." He stared at the unmoving tip of his rod. "You?"

"Yep. The whole ugly thing."

United by tragedy, the boys locked eyes.

"I hate bein' an orphan," Curtis said after a moment of silence. "Some folks act like you is made of glass; other folks act like you has a contagious disease. Either way, nobody wants to get too close, 'case it's catchin.'"

"I'm not an orphan. I have a new mother. Her name is Miss Emma Wright." Suddenly, his face lit up with a bright smile. He stood and started gathering his fishing supplies. "Get up," he told Curtis. "You're coming home with me."

"I can't do that! You're white, and I—"

"—And you don't have a family," Matt finished for him. "You're going to love Emma. She's beautiful, and she sings like an angel. And just wait 'til you taste her berry pie. She's making one for dessert tomorrow." Grinning, he gave Curtis a playful poke in the ribs. 'Course, you'll have to go to Sunday services and sing at the top of your lungs to earn a slice."

Curtis licked his lips. "I don't rightly recall when I last had any kind of pie."

The boys walked in companionable silence for a mile or so, kicking stones and crunching sticks beneath their boots, Matt carrying the fishing poles over one shoulder, and the wicker creel over the other, and Curtis dragging the half-empty pillow slip that held all his worldly possessions.

"Say," Curtis said after a time, "you never did tell me your name."

Holding out his hand in friendly greeting and lifting his chin, Matt threw back his shoulders. "Name's Matt. Matt Evans Wright." He turned Curtis's hand loose and pointed at the house directly in front of them. He led the way up the flagstone walk, singing "Emma" as he shoved open the front door. "Emma, we're home."

She stepped out of the kitchen, wiping her hands on a red-checkered tea towel. "We?"

"Me 'n' Curtis here," Matt said, aiming a thumb over his shoulder. "He's an orphan, too. I told him he could stay with us."

Emma's face did not register surprise. In the six months he'd been with her, Matt brought home a kitten, a dog, and a one-legged robin. What was one more little boy among the delightful menagerie? Jenni named the scruffy little cat Mouser, and since he found the bear-sized dog on the banks of the Patapsco, Matt called him

Pat. When the bird's stump healed, Emma would set him free. Meanwhile, Hoppy pecked contentedly in the birdcage that hung in a corner of the parlor.

"Curtis and I," she corrected, smiling gently. To Matt's friend, she said, "Hello, Curtis."

The child fidgeted nervously, and staring at the toes of his raggedy boots, said in a soft voice, "Hello, ma'am."

She slung the towel over one shoulder. "Tell him how things are, Matt," she said, hands on her hips.

The wide-eyed boy looked to Matt for guidance.

"Makes her feel old when folks call her 'ma'am'. Just call her 'Emma.' She likes that."

She relieved Matt of the creel and peered under its lid. "My, but aren't they two of the most beautiful rainbow trout you've ever seen!" She let the lid fall shut with a quiet slap. "While I'm getting these ready for the frying pan, I want you boys to wash up." Using her free hand as a duster, Emma added, "Run along, now. I have bread to knead."

"Curtis knows how to knead bread, Emma," Matt said.

She smiled gently. "Does he now?"

Curtis frowned at his new friend, and Matt explained: "He needs some bread right now. With jelly and butter on it. And so do I!"

Emma ruffled the boy's hair. "And I need the two of you to get washed up!"

Laughing, the boys bounded up the stairs. When they reached the landing, she called up the stairs, "Curtis, after your bath, Matt will get you a clean change of clothes. And Matt," she added, "see if maybe your old boots will fit Curtis."

As she started for the kitchen, she heard Curtis whimper, "Aw, do I really have to take a bath?"

"'Fraid so," came Matt's whispered response. "And I'll give you a little pointer."

"What?"

"Get used to hearing 'Cleanliness is next to godliness,' 'cause she says it a lot."

The two groaned in harmony, and Emma giggled as the parlor clock began its countdown toward noon. *Twenty-four hours till Sunday dinner*, she thought. Then, one hand over her chest, she bit her lower lip. *If your heart doesn't leap clean out of your chest first!*

⌒

Nate only owned one tie, and it had a gravy stain on it. He had two choices as he saw it: Go to Emma's dressed like a hobo, or endure his brother's good-natured teasing.

Wiggling his dark brows, Ian handed over a black string tie. "She's mighty easy on the eyes, I'll give you that much." He punctuated the comment with a mischievous wink. "All that lovely golden hair, and those eyes..." He whistled. "Why, they're bluer than the sky!"

"That'll be enough of that, Ian O'Neil," his wife scolded. "You'll have me thinkin' all your pretty words about me flashin' green eyes and fiery red hair were lies."

"Oh, but 'twas the truth, Mary me darlin', every last word!" Ian hugged her wife as close as her large, swollen belly would allow. In a loud whisper, he added, "I'm just tryin' to give me big brother a bit of encouragement; it's been an age since the man went a-courtin'!"

Mary wriggled free of her husband's warm embrace and turned to help her brother-in-law with his tie. "He's selective, is all. Isn't that right, Nate m'darlin'?"

"If I thought I could find a wife like you, sweet Mary," he said, smiling, "I'd snap her up so fast her eyes'd pop out of their sockets."

Finished with his tie, Mary affectionately patted Nate's chest. "Oh, go on with you now," she said on her way to the kitchen. "You'll have me head so big, I won't be fittin' through any of me doorways. Besides," she added, "I don't know as I'd like a sister-in-law with two big holes where her eyes used to be!"

Convinced she was out of earshot, Ian sidled up to Nate. "So tell me, big brother, does Da know you're takin' a meal with Emma Wright?"

"I'm thirty years old, Ian. I haven't asked Da's permission to visit a woman in nearly half my life." Running a finger under his now-tight collar, Nate winced. "What do you feed that wife of yours? She's strong as an ox!"

Laughing, Ian dropped a hand on his brother's shoulder. "I feed her huge doses of love and affection…" Narrowing one eye, he lowered his voice, "…spiced with just the right amount of sweet talk."

"So you'll not need an extra spoonful of sugar in your tea, then, will you, husband?" came the ladylike question from the kitchen.

The brothers stood staring in silence.

"Yes," Mary called through the wall, "I heard every word." She peeked around the corner to add, "You might consider a dash more of the pretty words the next time you're stirrin' up a batch of Happy Wife."

Nate pocketed both hands and looked around the room for something to focus on other than the warm, loving expression that connected Ian and Mary, though twenty feet separated them. He settled for his shoes. *Should've given 'em a quick shine*, he thought.

But his attire could not distract him from the thoughts pinging in his mind: He liked Emma Wright, liked her a lot. Ian was right: She was mighty easy on the eyes. She might be tall as a man, but everything else about her was one hundred percent woman.

While he was in Richmond, he was lucky enough to witness a field of bluebells in full bloom. It was, he thought at the time, the most beautiful sight he'd ever seen—a sea of pale blue, swaying in the wind. Emma's eyes reminded him of those bluebells, catching the sun and dancing with delight at every word spoken to her as those thick dark lashes fluttered in response.

He once rode through a wheat field, chasing down a runaway calf. If he had time to lean from the saddle and run his fingertips across those golden heads and silken spikes, it would likely have been like caressing velvet. Nate thought Emma's waist-length hair would probably feel like that.

And her skin! Against a background as creamy-white as vanilla ice cream, she had cheeks pinker than primrose petals, lightly dusted with tiny freckles. He'd attended a huge Virginia-style plantation wedding shortly before moving to Maryland, and when he'd leaned in to kiss the bride's cheek, he'd touched the shimmering sleeve of her gown. It couldn't possibly have been more satiny than Emma's skin.

For every wonderful trait that described her physical self, Emma had a dozen more that had nothing to do with outer beauty. She had a natural way about her that put folks immediately at ease. He'd heard many things about her in the months since he moved to Ellicott City, all of it good.

Take the way she cared for her aunt when the cancer came, for example, and the way she stepped right in and mothered little Jenni when Stella died. And the way Matt melted into her arms on that awful day, looking as haggard as any wounded man he'd seen on the battlefield. A few months with Emma had healed him, and put the little-boy shine back into the his horror struck blue eyes.

"Mark my words, this is the one."

"What're you goin' on about, Mary?" Ian asked.

She giggled. "He's so deep in thoughts of her; he's deaf, dumb, and blind, too!"

"How do you know it's Emma he's thinkin' about?"

"By that moon-eyed look on his face, Ian."

Their voices roused him from his reverie, and Nate blinked back to the present, only to find his brother and sister-in-law standing side by side, studying him intently.

Narrowing one mischief-making eye, Ian smirked and scratched his chin. "It's more a cow-eyed look, if you ask me."

Nate shrugged himself into a stern, controlled demeanor.

"Maybe it's 'cause she *moooves* him."

"Ian," Nate began.

"'Cause there's no *udder* girl for him."

"That's enough, Ian," said the older brother. "Thank you for the use of the tie," he added, walking to the door. "I'll get it back soon as—"

"Why don't you keep it?" Ian winked at Mary, then said, "A man has to wear a tie to his own weddin', after all."

Mary waddled up and opened the door. "Be on your way, now, or you'll be late." Hustling him onto the porch, she shook a maternal finger at him. "There's nothin' ruder than a tardy dinner guest." Giving him one last, playful shove, she patted her round tummy. "It'd be nice if I could bounce your little ones on my knee before I'm too old."

Mary's smile faded. She stood on the first step, he on the ground, putting them eye to eye. One hand on his shoulder, she looked deep into his eyes. "You've tortured yourself long enough, Nathan O'Neil. What's done is done, and I'll have no more of it, you hear!"

It'll never be done, he told her silently. *Nor can the results be undone.* Mary had always been insightful and intuitive, but she couldn't read the secrets written on his heart. Nate thanked God for that, because what would he have left if Mary lost faith in him!

He couldn't love this tiny, spunky woman more if she was born an O'Neil. The fondness he felt for her glowed in his eyes when he said, "You must have a heart the size of your head, darlin' woman, to care so deeply for a man as flawed as me."

She laid a hand upon his bearded cheek. "You're no more flawed than the next man, Nate. You've got to start believin' that." Then, as if sensing his dour mood, she stood straighter, and smiled brightly as the maternal finger wagged again. "Mark my words," she said. "Emma's the one!"

Hands deep in his pockets, Nate rolled Mary's words over in his mind as he walked the mile to Emma's house. Could his sister-in-law be right? Might Emma be the one? Was it possible that, even when she knew every ugly part of his past, she could love him?

Nate shook his head. Impossible! What woman could love a man who caused the needless deaths of nearly a hundred men! *Eighty-seven to be exact,* he thought bitterly; *four score and seven lives ago, I was once a man. Could I ever redress such an evil?* he wondered. *My Gettysburg redress,* he added ruefully.

Emma deserved a whole man, not one broken by guilt. She deserved sunshine, no matter the weather, and rainbows, and flowers.

He was never one for childish wishing. But he wished now that it was summertime, or springtime at least, so he could bring her a handful of flowers. There was her house, not fifty yards ahead, but not even a winter-crisped dandelion to pluck. Nate stood at the end of the road, staring at the tidy white-picketed porch, flanked by black-shuttered windows, and in those windows, lacy curtains, like those that hung in so many of the thatched cottages dotting the Irish countryside before famine and fever made paupers and beggars of his people.

And behind those curtains, Emma. Perhaps she was stirring a pot on the stove, fussing over the bow of her apron, or poking a log on the fire. Somehow, he just knew she was the type who'd give even the most mundane task her complete and undivided attention. Might he actually hope he would someday receive her complete and undivided attention?

Nate sighed. If he a shred of decency left in him, he would turn around and walk away. He'd head for his shop and lock himself in. It might hurt her feelings, when she found she'd been stood up. *Better that than have a bum like you as part of her life!*

But something seemed to be drawing him, pulling him towards that tiny, two-story house, and before he knew it, Nate found himself walking up the path and climbing the stairs. He knocked on the windowed front door.

The curtain rustled, and her smiling face peered through the glass, as though she were genuinely pleased to see him! Nate's heart beat fast...odd, since time itself seemed to have slowed to a crawl. The brass knob turned slowly, and the door opened bit by bit.

It's not too late, he considered, *to beg off. Make up some excuse, and—*

"It's so good to see you," she said, opening the door wide. Her musical voice caressed his ears like a mother's hand soothes her fretting babe, and Nate willingly followed the delicious sound of it, smiling and nodding like a buffoon in response to her happy chatter.

Does she realize what she is doing? he wondered. Did she understand that her friendly greeting had done more than invite him inside? Was she aware that, as she plumped the parlor sofa cushions and poured a cup of hot tea to warm him and make him feel cozy and comfortable, she had succeeded! Or had it simply been an accident of fate, some curious coincidence that her glittering eyes and lovely smile told him he would always be welcome, and wanted, and accepted here, despite his despicable past?

Being in her presence was, for Nate, like feeling the sunshine on his face after a week of cloudy skies; she was the rainbow that came after the rain.

She deserved a strong man.

God blessed him with a good, strong body, and in gratitude, Nate used it to its fullest potential, felling huge oaks and hefting the logs as though they were saplings. He feared he paid so much attention to exercising his body that he forgot to exercise his spirit, resulting in weakness—weakness that made him turn to the sharp taste of whiskey that dulled the pain of war, and weakness that drove him to drink himself into oblivion on the battlefield that night terrible night.

Weakness held him spellbound in her parlor, sipping tea like a proper gentleman caller, making small talk as they waited for the Sunday roast to come out of the oven.

And weakness would bring him back, as often and for as long as Emma would allow it.

THREE

Emma found it an especially attractive character trait that Nate seemed not to notice Curtis's skin was considerably darker than Matt and Jenni's. They were children in his eyes, it was as simple as that, and that's the way he treated them.

She suspected that not all of Ellicott City's so-called "good" Christians would react to her ready-made family as matter-of-factly as Nate had. No doubt there would be those who'd curl their lips with shock and dismay to know she willingly took a homeless Negro boy into her house with every intent of calling him "son" in the future. And when the children went out to play after dinner, she said as much to Nate.

"'Tis true the war's over," he whispered, "but some folks are still fightin' the same old battles." Absentmindedly, he picked at a nub in the linen tablecloth. "It's easy to say that God loves us all equally, whatever we look like; it's another matter entirely to live it."

That he read what was written on her heart touched her deeply, and Emma reached out and laid her hands atop one of his.

"Too many of us take for granted how easily we're accepted as we go from place to place. If only more people could be like you."

He frowned slightly. *Cowards and shirkers? We've more'n enough of those in the world already!* he thought. But what he said was, "You don't know what you're talkin' about, Emma."

Shaking her head, Emma pressed on. "I know exactly what I'm talking about. You really understand the true meaning of the word 'equality,' and I have a feeling it has very little to do with the fact that you and your family experienced prejudice at the hands of the English: You'd be this same man even if the O'Neils had been on American soil for a hundred years."

His frown gentled as a smile lit his dark eyes. "Speakin' of understandin'…" He sandwiched her hands between his own. "Not many folks understand what it was like in Ireland. What it's still like, and what it'll likely be like a hundred years from now…if there are any Irish left by then." Nodding, he gave her fingers a little squeeze. "Aye, it could be said that the Irish were slaves to the English. Unfortunately for the ascendancy, they're runnin' out of space."

"English," Emma said wryly. "You know, according to my late aunt, you are English."

His brows dipped low in the center of his forehead. "Me? English!"

She nodded. "Aunt Stella was Amish; to her people, anyone who wasn't German was a Brit."

Smiling, Nate shook his head. "Well, now, don't that beat all. Me, English!"

She tilted her head slightly, and admired the wide-open honesty in his eyes. It was a strong, manly face of angles and planes—from ruddy-red cheeks to the patrician nose to a broad, bearded chin—that might have been sculpted by Michelangelo, Donatello, or Bernini.

On their last wedding anniversary, Ronald Anderson gave his wife a mink wrap, and at the formal dinner party the couple threw to celebrate ten years together, Joetta let Emma try it on. She would never forget the luxurious feel of the mahogany-colored fur as it brushed her neck and cheeks, as she stroked it with her palms. Nate's collar-length hair would be softer still, she believed.

Emma never felt more alive or at peace than when walking in the woods during a light summer rain, when the downy moss underfoot glowed emerald and the bark of each tree took on a charcoal hue. A wisp of mist here, swirling around the ankles, a patch of fog there, hovering about the shoulders, and raindrops glistening from each pine needle turned the ordinary world into an enchanted fairyland that could cool and calm her even on the most frazzling days. Looking into Nate's wide brown eyes gave Emma that same sense of serenity.

She appreciated the hard work that had chiseled his barrel-chested, burly build. He worked with planes and saws and awls all day, and had the powerfully big, calloused hands to prove it, yet he touched her hand as if it were made of delicate crystal, and tousled the children's hair as gently as he might if they were but babes in arms.

Emma liked to think of herself as well-balanced and independent: She could chop wood like a lumberjack, and cook like a fancy French chef. She handled a horse like a jockey, and sewed circles around most women in Howard County. Being adept with both musket and bow, she took down her share of whitetails and cooked them up with finesse. While a few suitors found her aptness admirable, most found the gifts anything but admirable. Several said she talked too much. Some complained she didn't say enough. One thing rang true in all cases: Emma, at five foot seven, was simply too tall to suit their taste in women.

But her height didn't seem to faze Nate. She guessed him at five foot nine; certainly not a small man, but not a giant, either. How he measured up by the rule had nothing whatsoever to do with the fact that in her eyes, Nate O'Neil was by far the biggest man she had ever met.

He'd definitely got off on the right foot by rescuing Matt that day, thundering into town on a great black steed like the proverbial knight in shining armor, risking life and limb to save an innocent child. *"Greater love hath no man,"* Scripture said. Emma never saw love of this depth before.

There was more to his charm than the heroic deed, but she couldn't single out any particular characteristic. Was it the way his eyes glittered when he smiled, or his sparkling wit? Could it be his way of drumming home his points by tapping the table, or the euphonic timbre of his Irish brogue? Emma couldn't say.

"And from what I hear," he was saying, "it's not much better today than 'twas when we left Ireland. 'Tis a sad an' shameful thing to see your homeland, erodin' right before your very eyes."

What else had he said as she sat, mesmerized by his presence? Emma worried. She could only hope the sighs and murmurs she distractedly uttered had been the appropriate responses to his words. Anything else, and Nate might get the impression that he bored her, and the truth was, she found him endlessly fascinating!

"Do you have any plans to return to Ireland?"

"America is m'home now." He smiled. "Though I wouldn't mind goin' back for a visit." He let go of one of her hands to take a sip of his coffee. "I think you'd like Ireland." The cup clattered when he returned it to the saucer. "And Ireland would like you."

She mirrored his playful smile. "Why? Do I seem to be the type who'd be intrigued by the 'little people'?"

"Not likely," he admitted, chuckling. "If you're any 'type' at all, it's the type that isn't fooled by magical tales. You seem to me a practical lass who knows what's what, who speaks her mind." Both brows rose as he added, "There's quite a lot about you to admire, Emma Wright."

Her heart flipped and her stomach flopped. It was as if she were experiencing an allover blush in response to his admiration. *Admiration,* she thought, *admirable as it is, it's hardly romantic!*

And Emma needed a bit of romance in her life.

Dear Lord in heaven, Emma prayed, *if marriage is among Your plans for me, let it be to this wonderful man!*

The clock struck four.

The children had gone outside to play shortly before two. She and Nate had been talking like old friends for so long, the grease coagulated around the beef roast. "Four o'clock. I can't believe how quickly time passed!" she said, sliding her hands from beneath his.

Immediately, Emma regretted the action. His palms, warm and dry, felt comforting, like a blanket that protected her from the chilly February air. "Goodness," she said, rising and heading for the fireplace. "I haven't stoked the fire in hours. It'll be a minor miracle if there are coals enough to keep it going." She was rambling and she knew it, but seemed powerless to stanch the nonsensical flow of words. "I hope Matt brought in an arm load of wood, as I asked him to, because—"

"Emma," Nate said calmly, standing in her path, "I've been sittin' there for nearly two hours, tryin' to think of a polite way to put it, but..."

Giggling, she covered her mouth with one hand. "I do go on, don't I? You'll have to forgive me; sometimes I just don't know when to—"

"'Twas I who did most of the talkin', darlin' Emma." Gently, Nate chucked her under the chin. "You're a fine listener, that you are, but what I was thinkin' had nothin' to do with who said what."

Emma cupped her elbows and waited. Would he say, as so many before him had, that while he found her to be a likable sort, they simply weren't a good match? Or would he confess, as several of her suitors had, that he pretty well resigned himself to the bachelor's life? She bit her lower lip to still its trembling. *Lord,* she prayed on a sigh, *give me the strength to get through yet another rejection, 'cause I'm no spring chicken, y'know!*

"I've been sittin' here tryin' to remember when I last wanted to kiss a woman the way I want to kiss you," he said, pulling her into his arms. "And the answer is, I don't think I've ever wanted to kiss a woman as I want to kiss you."

She swallowed the little gasp of surprise that threatened to pop from her throat. His face moved slowly closer. When he came so near that he was completely out of focus, she closed her eyes, held her breath, and waited.

Oh, she'd been kissed a time or two, and found them pleasant experiences. But neither encounter could even begin to compare to this!

It was more, so much more than Nate's lips, pressed to hers. It seemed they became one living, breathing being, united in heart and mind and soul by a thing as innocent as a kiss. She knew, as she stood in the protective circle of his arms, that near him was where she wanted to spend the rest of her days. And she knew, too, as his hard-pounding heart thrummed against her, that Nate was a man capable of living and loving to the fullest—to the end.

She hadn't realized how lonely her spirit had been 'til he pressed her close. Oh how glorious it felt to be wanted by this handsome, heroic man! Her heart pounded with passion, and sang for joy, and praised God, all at the same time.

They stood so near that not so much as a spring breeze could have passed between them, yet she yearned to be nearer still. Emma's fingers inched up his broad shoulders and slipped slowly behind his neck, then combed through the thick hair that curved and curled above his collar. Just as she'd expected…the texture of silk and satin. Exhaling a whispery sigh, she basked in the warmth of the moment.

Suddenly, Emma sensed a strange tension between them. A quiet groan rumbled through him as he stepped back and, holding her at arm's length, bored into her eyes with an intensity that would melt metal.

"I...I'm sorry," he rasped, averting his eyes. "Forgive me for bein' so bold and forward. I never meant you any disrespect, Emma; I haven't any excuse that'll do, so I'll offer none."

As she read the regret on his face, his misery became hers. Seeing him in such a state made her heart ache, and the only thought in her head at the moment was easing his discomfort. "Nate," she whispered, a finger over his lips. "Shhh. It's all right. There's no need to apolo—"

"I got caught up in the moment, I'm afraid," he said as if she hadn't spoken at all. "Got pulled in by the warmth of the room." He met her eyes. "Got pulled in by the warmth of your smile." Shaking his head sadly, he added, "And, oh, but it's a warm smile, darlin' Emma."

She studied his dusky chocolate-brown eyes. She sensed all along that he'd been deeply scarred by some tragic event. The proof was written all over his face, in the way he stood, stiff-backed and rigid. Perhaps a careless woman had broken his heart. Maybe he'd been the heartbreaker, and felt guilty about it still.

Yes, his agony went deep—to the marrow of his bones and to the core of his heart. However he came by the injury to his soul, Nate had not yet healed. But he might, given time and patience and love, and someone who cared enough to give him all three.

She cared...probably more than was healthy so early in their relationship. Emma had to face the possibility that if she gave her heart to this man whom life bruised and battered—though it would not be a deliberate act, or one born of maliciousness—he might just hand back her heart in a jumble of pieces.

On the other hand, it could just as easily go the other way. Only time would tell.

She would give him that time, starting now.

Emma's hands still rested on his shoulders, and she gave Nate a playful shake. "I have a confession to make," she said, lifting her chin, "I hope you won't think me a...a wanton trollop for saying...

for admitting that I wanted that kiss every bit as much as you did."

His eyes widened with surprise, and the corners of his mouth turned up in the beginnings of a smile.

She gave a nod of her head and grinned mischievously. "So now that we've both apologized, perhaps you'll be so kind as to help me clear the table."

⌒

When Curtis had been part of the family for nearly two months, Emma told him, "You fit in this family like a hand in a glove." To which Matt had responded, "Yeah…a kid glove!" It was just that sort of lightheartedness that abounded since Curtis became a regular member of the household. An eager-to-please child, he did more than his fair share of the chores, a trait Matt and Jenni quickly learned to appreciate.

As the days turned to weeks and the weeks to months, he began feeling a welcome addition to the unique family unit, and proved it by telling jokes and playing tricks that made the children's laughter as much a part of day-to-day life as their tears had once been.

She loved him dearly, and never wanted to let him go. Then the director of the new college at Rock Hill heard about Emma's newest orphan, and made a special trip to the clinic to talk with her about Curtis. She was in Doctor Farley's office, tidying files, when he rapped at the door.

Though she'd seen him in church before, Emma had never been formally introduced to the man. He took care of that by removing his tall black hat and bowing at the waist. "Brother Aphrates," he said, smiling stiffly, "and I've come to speak on a friend's behalf. His name is Jedidiah Jones, and he recently purchased a small mill in Elk Ridge," Aphrates explained. "He hopes to do a good business with the Negroes of the area. He's married, of course, and a devout Christian; one of the most respectable men I know."

Nodding politely, Emma could not for the life of her under-stand why she should be the recipient of so much information about a man she'd never met, however good and decent he might be. Aphrates must have read the question in her eyes, for he said, "In the fifteen years they've been together, Jed and his wife have had no children."

So that's it, Emma thought. *The man wants Curtis.* "You say he's a good and decent man, then why doesn't he come himself to discuss the...adoption?"

The brother blanched. "You do go straight to the heart of a matter, don't you, Miss Wright?"

She folded her hands primly in front of her. "I find it saves invaluable time for everyone concerned. Now, why isn't Mr. Jones here himself?"

"Jed hasn't been a free man long enough to trust white folks' reaction to him. He was afraid you might not want to talk to him."

"Why? Because he's a Negro?"

The brother nodded, and Emma frowned. She started to com-plain that she'd never judged anyone in her life, especially for a reason as superficial as the color of their skin! But how could Mr. Jones know that? "I'm sure your friend is as fine a man as you say, Brother Aphrates, but—"

"I'm glad you agree!" he interrupted. "The boy will be better off with his own kind," he began, nodding. "He'll be so much hap-pier in a home where he's loved and accepted for what he is, instead of..." He shrugged.

But Emma *did* love and accept Curtis for what he was, because she truly believed that God created all humans from the bones of Adam; all mankind was Curtis's "own kind"! Emma's frown turned into a scowl. "Instead of what?" she demanded, hands on her hips now.

Aphrates' cheeks flushed brightly as he shuffled nervously from one foot to the other. "I only meant...that is...er..."

"What I was about to say, sir, is that while I'm certain your friend is everything you say he is, I'd have to see for myself before I agree to discuss the matter of adoption."

"Please forgive me, Miss Wright. I never intended any disrespect or insult. I only presumed you'd prefer dealing with me, as Mr. Jones' representative, rather than having the orphans' court intervene."

She swallowed a gasp. *Orphans' court? What reason would they have to…?* But Emma knew she was not Curtis's mother, and with no paperwork stating that she had legally assumed the role, if the matter was brought before a judge…

"My only concern," she said, biting back her fear, "is Curtis's well-being."

"It's patently obvious you care a great deal for the boy," the brother said. "These are hard times, yet you've shared what little you have to make a good Christian home for these orphans." He smiled warmly. "I admire you greatly."

Admire. On the night they'd had dinner at her house, the word had not been romantic when Nate said it, and in her mind, it wasn't complimentary coming from this brother, either; Emma hadn't taken the youngsters into her home to be admired. She'd done it because they needed her, and frankly, she needed them!

But it was Curtis's needs she would focus on now, not her own. "I wouldn't put my hand in a gopher hole without looking around first, to make sure it's safe, and Curtis is far dearer to me than my hand." She quirked a brow to add, "Perhaps you'd be so kind as to arrange a meeting between Curtis and the Joneses to see if he takes to them."

Aphrates shook Emma's hand. "I'd be happy to," he said. "I'll send a note as soon as I set something up."

What if Curtis *did* take to them! Suddenly, she felt the urge to cry. But she squared her shoulders and nodded. "Thank you."

He turned to leave, but hesitated in the doorway. "I'll understand if you choose not to mention this to anyone in the interim. No point in needlessly giving the boy any sleepless nights."

"Thank you," she said again.

When he was gone, she didn't return to her filing. Instead, Emma sat at Doctor Farley's desk and wept.

FOUR

After three solid days of hard labor, Nate completed the huge wooden tub that would sit in Amos Hudson's pasture, collecting rainwater for his cows. It took Nate, Ian, and two powerful farm horses to guide the gigantic half-barrel onto Nate's work sled for delivery to Amos's farm.

He didn't mind the hard work, for as long as there was a tool in his hand, Nate could focus on the methods and materials to complete a job rather than on the misery of his past. There was a nobility to the work that stood in stark contrast to the life he led in the past—a bit of comfort from distressing memories.

He relived that bloody night thousands of times in his dreams, but there was no face-to-face reminder until yesterday morning.

Nate was in the general store, buying sweets for his sister's children, when he saw a huge hulking man exit the feed and grain across the street. He looked again and squinted, unable to believe his eyes. There was something familiar about the man's smug, self-assured swagger. Only one man would clothe himself from neck to ankles in fringed buckskin: Hank Campbell.

Nate strove to keep a careful check on his emotions at all times. If anyone paid any mind to his rigid back, or his tight-lipped expression, he'd pass it off as concentration. "Just plottin' the layout of me next job," he'd explain, a mere hint of a smile in his eyes. He would not, could not let them see into his heart, for to do that would be to allow them to see what he really was: a no-good drunkard who'd killed nearly a hundred men. Now, every muscle tightened and every nerve stood on end as this walking, talking echo from his past sauntered toward the bank.

Questions plagued him, and Nate ground his molars together, seeking answers. Hank claimed to have been born and raised in Nashville, and confessed that, if he survived the war, he intended to head straight home to work the family farm. Why on earth was he here in Ellicott City, and how long would he stay?

Another man might have given Hank at least half the blame for what happened that night, but Nate knew where the real blame belonged. If Hank knew how Nate shirked his duties, would he speak of it here, in the town Nate's family decided to make their permanent home?

"That'll be twenty-nine cents," the widow Henderson said.

But Nate did not hear the elderly woman, for yet another inescapable fact set his pulse to pounding like war drums in his ears: Hank wouldn't be loading sacks of flour and sugar onto the buckboard near the feed and grain unless he planned to stay a good long time.

"Mr. O'Neil?"

Mrs. Dixon sidled up beside him to pay for her own groceries. Rolling her eyes at the shopkeeper, she gave Nate a gentle elbow in the ribs.

Forcing himself to look away from Hank, who'd just untethered his horse, Nate glanced around, as if trying to determine who had touched him and why. "Mmmm?"

Dumping her purchases unceremoniously on the counter, Mrs. Dixon sighed, and with a nod of her head, indicated the widow. "She's waiting."

It was all he could do to look from Mrs. Dixon's face to the widow's, for the man in buckskin was climbing onto the wagon seat. *And headed where?* Nate wondered.

Both women wore the patient yet scolding expression of a schoolmarm who'd just heard "the dog ate my homework." *She's waiting?* he asked himself. *Waiting for what?*

And then he noticed Mrs. Henderson's hand, palm up and fingers wiggling. "Twenty-nine cents," she said, carefully enunciating every word, as though speaking to a very young...or a very stupid boy.

"Aye. Of course." He poked through his coin pouch. "How much do I owe you?"

Both gray brows furrowed and shaking her head, she leaned across the counter. "Twenty-nine cents! I could write it down for you, if you like."

With trembling hands, Nate distractedly counted out several coins and dropped them into her upturned palm, and taking the small paper sack she held, he nodded. "Thank you, ma'am." Sidestepping clumsily toward the door, he touched a finger to his brow. "You ladies have yourselves a nice day now, y'hear?"

"Must've thumped his noggin on one of those contraptions in his shop," he heard the widow say as he stepped onto the porch.

"Either that, or his hat's too tight," Mrs. Dixon agreed.

If only thumpin' your head was the reason you're in the shape you're in, Nate said to himself. He could have lived quite nicely with the consequences of a head injury. *'Tis your conscience that's been thumpin' you since that night,* he added, *and it'll never let you be.*

He was in no mood to visit his sister. Her children would have to wait until tomorrow for their candy. Perhaps by then, his head would be cleared enough to good-naturedly endure their childish pranks and jokes. Perhaps tomorrow, he'd be ready to scoop them up in a big hug when they came tearing down the path shouting, "Uncle Nate! Uncle Nate!" For the moment, he needed to be alone. *You've more'n enough to keep you busy,* he thought, *gettin' Buster Russel's sled ready for delivery.*

Earlier that morning, Buster stopped him on the way into the general store. "How long will it take to build me a sled like yours?"

"Two, three days," he'd said, shrugging.

"Will ten dollars cover the labor and materials?" Buster wanted to know, sliding several bills from his pocket.

"It would," Nate admitted, "but two dollars will be more than enough to buy the materials. You can give me the rest when I see you're happy with the work."

Nodding, Buster handed him two bills and put the rest of his money away. "No rush, mind you, but I'm headin' west soon as the weather warms a bit." Staring at some unknown spot beyond Nate's shoulder, he added in an absentminded, faraway voice, "Always figured Cora would outlive me. Never gave a moment's thought to what life would be like if she went first."

A stray dog raced by in hot pursuit of a mangy cat, rousing Buster from his reverie. Immediately, he lit into his plan: "Gonna build me a cabin in the Blue Ridge Mountains. Ain't gonna need much in the way of creature comforts, and I'll earn more'n enough to buy what I need by trappin' fox and beaver up there."

The men shook hands and parted company, and Nate headed inside to begin construction of Buster's sled. For jobs like this, he'd combed the woods near Oella, searching for good strong oaks with enough gnarl to make sled runners. He poked through his stack of wood, and chose two posts with suitably upturned ends as he thought of his afternoon at Emma's.

The children gathered around him as if he were old Saint Nick himself, chattering like chipmunks, each doing their part to make him feel at home. He'd always liked children, and before the war, thought once that he and Laura might bring half a dozen young ones into the world. If Nate hadn't broken off the engagement, would his love for Laura have grown...and hers for him?

Nate doubted it. First and foremost, "affection" more aptly described his feelings for his delicate little ex-fiancé. He rather liked the way she gushed with gratitude when he brought her a trinket, a box of candy, or a bouquet of flowers. And the way she giggled girlishly as he carried her over a mud puddle, or lifted her down from the wagon. Taking care of her made him feel strong, and manly, and needed.

She was blessed with an ample supply of feminine grace and charm, but whatever ingredient made a woman see that even a strong, stoic man like himself could do with a hit of pampering now and then was not in her. Laura had taken great joy in accepting every gift and gentlemanly mannerism Nate doled out, but never gave a thought to his joy. It wouldn't have taken much to show him that she cared...a kind word now and then to acknowledge his kindness, a batch of sugar cookies for his birthday, something cool to quench his thirst on a hot summer afternoon....

He didn't expect any woman could be the wife his mother own ma had been. Every day, no matter how late his father came in from the fields, she'd come running and throw her arms around him, and anyone could see that she was truly pleased to see him. One look at his face, and she knew exactly what kind of day he had. Then she'd feed him a piping hot bowl of stew and stand behind his chair as he ate, massaging his shoulders as she chattered about the events of her own workday.

To love a man as his mother had loved his father, a woman would need a heart as big as her head. And most women, in his experience, were exactly like Laura. Oh, she'd done him a few kindnesses in the months they were betrothed, but it hadn't taken a genius to see the deeds had quickly lost their luster once the *quid pro quo* found its mate. In that way, Laura would be a girl until she drew her last breath. And a girl simply didn't have it in her to look away from her own needs long enough to see to her man's.

In many ways, Emma reminded him of his dear mother. He could see his ma in the way Emma tended her orphans. And when she stood in the circle of his embrace and he broke off their kiss, Emma had searched his face, just as his mother searched his father's every evening for signs that would explain his distress.

Emma was feisty, and he liked that, because it told him that her grit told him was born of a mind set that compelled her to meet life head-on. When he pulled out her chair at the table, she'd nodded politely and thanked him. And later, when he returned from refilling the biscuit basket, she'd pulled out *his* chair and said in her smiling, matter-of-fact way that "Polite respect doesn't come in pink or blue. It simply *is*."

If not for the war and what happened that night, he would probably have married Laura. Certainly, he would have remained true to his promise to love and keep her for better or for worse, but he had a strong suspicion their marriage would accent the "worse" of the vow rather than the "better." A mutually satisfying union, he'd always contended, needed more to sustain it than fondness, however genuine. It needed full-blown, no-holds-barred, all-out love, like the kind his parents shared.

Buster and Cora had shared that kind of love, too, and like his parents', it had grown stronger with each test of time, like iron, tempered by the red-hot fire of his forge. Before Cora's death, Buster had greeted friend, neighbor, and stranger with a broad, contagious smile that seemed to start deep inside him, the way heat radiates from the glowing coals in a potbellied stove, warming and inviting folks to draw near. But without his Cora, Nate couldn't help but notice that Buster's friendly warmth had cooled; like a fire with no one to stoke it, the heat inside him slowly faded.

Oh, Buster could claim to be heading for the mountains to escape the city's crowds and noise, but Nate knew better. Loneliness drove him west, and it would be loneliness that would smother the life from his soul. Was it so terrible, really, to move on to the next world, even a bit before one's time, after having shared a love like that? Nate's heart ached for the sad-eyed old fellow.

He kept his pity to himself, however, for Buster no doubt believed folks were buying his "take it all in stride" attitude. For Nate to lay hand upon shoulder, or offer a sympathetic word, would force the grizzled old man to admit that his grief ran so deep that it could be measured by everyone he met. Buster had earned this time of respite and respect, and Nate would not throw cold water on the man's fading fire.

He wondered if he would ever experience such a love—a love that would have him waking each morning, thrilled by the prospect of spending yet another day with his beloved. Nate didn't think so. Not when he had nothing to offer a woman but the after-effects of his dastardly deed. Still, he yearned for the quiet comfort that comes from a lifelong love.

If not for the war, that dreadful, deadly war...

Nate shook the cobwebs of despair from his mind and aimed his full concentration on the work at hand. By day's end, Buster would have the best-built sled this side of the Mississippi!

Even on a bright and sunny summer day, the interior of his barn-like shop was shady and cool, but in these chill winds of mid-March, the air seemed laced with ice. The heat of the forge warmed him as he lit the first of four whale-oil lanterns hanging from pegs above his worktable. Nate averted his eyes from the coals glowing in the bowels of the oven, not to protect them from being singed, but because the fire reminded him too much of that bloody, blazing night.

Cranking the big-toothed black wheel, he allowed water to enter the turbine. "Easy now," he said to himself, "Not too much to start off." Later, for more energy to operate his saws and drills, he'd give the wheel several more turns, inviting a heavier flow that would set the belts and pulleys that powered the tools to snap and roll into creaky motion.

He laid a leather template flat on the table and, with a lead pencil, drew a line around the rough-cut runner. Water all but gushed through the turbine now, and as the belts flapped and the pulleys groaned, the wicked teeth of the saw blade glinted in the lamplight, as the bones of his fallen comrades had gleamed in the moonlight.

Keep your mind on your work, he reprimanded himself, *or they'll be sweepin' your fingers up with the sawdust!*

Nate loosed the brake that set the saw spinning. Then guiding the runner past the blade, he sliced a forty-five degree bevel down both sides of the ten-foot length of wood. Trial and error taught him to use the first runner as a template for the second to prevent the sled from cutting right or left as it whispered through the snow.

Turning both now-flared runners upside down, Nate secured them to the sled's crossbeams using iron bolts and then nailed down the side-by-side decking planks. He noticed how the wood was the same honey-gold color as the coffins of his fellow soldiers.

A surge of self-loathing for what he did to cause their grisly deaths jolted through him, giving him the might to flip the heavy sled upside down. Stamping angrily on the bellows pedal, he gave the hissing coals in the bottom of the forge enough air to burn with bluish-green flames.

Wearing thick leather gloves, he slid a ten foot length of two-inch wide and half-inch thick steel from a pile, and thrust one end into the furnace, turning it over and over, until both sides glared cherry red. Quickly, he slapped it flat against the wooden runner's sole, squinting into the smoke that spiraled toward his nostrils as the scarlet-hot shoe's tongues of flame hissed and spit upon the runner.

He pounded with all his might, jaw clenched and lips thinned with grim determination in the hopes that the steady clang-clank of hammer to shoe would drown out the sounds that seemed to hang from the trees the night after the Yankee attack—the hiss and pop of rifle butts, tent poles, and canteens burning in the fires they set to destroy their enemies' encampment—and the anguished groans of dying Rebel soldiers.

After he shaped the shoe to the runner's configuration, he picked up a small oaken water bucket and doused the glowing seal, quenching its thirsty fire. If only his thirst for redemption could be quenched so easily! Nate believed guilt would burn forever in him, like the hot shoe smoked against the timbers of the runners.

The cold seeped through the cracks between the rough-hewn walls. Nate was chilled to the bone, and tired. He was more tired than he cared to admit as he installed the flat-head bolts that fastened the shoes to the runners. Tomorrow, he would hitch his team to the sled and haul it over to Buster's place. Tonight, he would pray for sleep to rescue him from the ghosts of that humid Chattanooga night.

Nate gathered a hefty arm load of firewood and turned off three of the lanterns. He carried the fourth up the plain board steps that led to his sparsely furnished room, and placed it in the center of a small wooden table.

Hunger and weariness battled in his head. Lethargy won out, and he laid upon his bunk. Whiskey was responsible for his craven behavior that agonizing night, and still he wanted it! To avoid temptation, he'd poured the contents of the bottle stashed behind his cot into the river, and did likewise with the one stored in the rafters. But there was one left...hidden in the floorboards.

"No!" he bellowed, face and fists aimed at the rafters. "You'll not give in to its lure!"

The order was no sooner out of his mouth than he got to his feet, dropped to his knees, and pried up the loose board. And there it lay, gleaming in the lamplight like liquid gold, singing his name like a saloon girl croons to drunks in a pub. Hovering there on his hands and knees, Nate hung his head. *Lord God*, he prayed, *Lord God Almighty, give me strength.*

With a groan, he replaced the board and got back into bed. Matthew 6:9–13 brought him peace on many other nights like this, when the temptation called and the terrible dream threatened him. Nate closed his eyes and in a hoarse, pain-threaded whisper, began reciting, *"Our Father which art in heaven, hallowed be Thy name. Thy kingdom come. Thy will be done in earth, as it is in heaven. Give us this day our daily bread. And forgive us our debts, as we forgive our debtors..."*

Will I ever know forgiveness? Nate wondered. Could he be forgiven the debt of so many lives?

"And lead us not into temptation, but deliver us from evil...." The bottle was Nate's evil, and though he hadn't tasted the fiery elixir in nearly a year, it called to him, still.

"For thine is the kingdom, and the power, and the glory, forever. Amen."

Tears burned behind his lids, but he did not blink them away. As they slipped silently from the corners of his eyes, Nate slid into a hard and vengeful slumber.

∽

The person on the other side of the door knocked twice, hesitated, knocked three more times. Suspicious, despite having heard the signal, Aubrey Farley peered through the lacy curtains, and saw a man wearing a fringed deerskin jacket, a Confederate-gray fez perched jauntily on his head.

Dimming the lantern's flame, he opened the door a crack and whispered, "I thought I told you to wait 'til midnight to—"

"It's a cold night," the man bit out, "and I've been riding since Saturday. Now let me in, or the deal's off."

When the door opened a bit, he stepped boldly inside. "Nice place you've got here, Doc," he said, nodding approvingly as he glanced around the room. Pocketing both hands in trousers that matched his buckskin coat, he strode nonchalantly into the parlor. "Yessiree, a real nice place." Looking over his shoulder, he grinned. "If this is what a college education can buy a man, maybe I should've left the army to go to medical school."

And before the doctor had a chance to respond, he licked his lips and slapped his palms together. "I sure could use some grub and a jigger of whiskey." The smile died a quick death as he added, "I've been riding since Saturday, don't forget."

"Wipe that smirk off your face, Campbell. This isn't a social call."

With the calm deliberation of a preacher opening his hymnal on Sunday morning, Campbell unholstered a six-shooter and balanced it on the palm of one big hand. "Ever used one of these, Doc?" he asked, admiring its gleaming silver barrel.

"I should say not. I am a pacifist, I'll have you know!"

Campbell's dark eyes narrowed dangerously as a snarl curled his upper lip. "Since when?"

Farley said nothing.

"Pacifist, my foot! That's a load of hogwash, and we both know it." In a heartbeat, he whirled the gun around until the gun's bright pearl handle disappeared into his meaty fist.

The doctor's eyes widened in response to the *whir-tick-tick* of the gun's spinning chamber, widened further still when Campbell squinted one eye to sight the pistol in. "Put that thing down, you idiot," Farley scolded, feigning a courage not reflected in his eyes, "before you shoot someone and—"

"Maybe," Campbell growled, "shootin' someone is exactly what I have in mind." He aimed at the doctor's forehead. "Revolver like this can take down an elk if you know where to aim…" One corner of his mustached upper lip lifted in an evil grin. "…and I know where to aim."

Blanching, Farley yanked the red silk scarf from his vest pocket and blotted his perspiring brow. "Perhaps there is some ham left from supper...in the kitchen." Turning to leave, he added, "Now for the last time, put that foul thing away. And keep your voice down or you'll wake the missus."

Campbell fell into step beside him and, as they rounded the corner, draped his arm over Farley's shoulder. Pressing the gun barrel to the doctor's temple, he said under his breath, "You listen to me, Aubrey, and you listen good: You ever call me an idiot again, it'll be the last word out of your newly pacifist mouth." And as if he hadn't made the murderous threat at all, he grinned. Using the gun as a pointer now, he indicated the door at the end of the hall. "That the kitchen? I sure hope so, 'cause I'm starving."

The last time Aubrey Farley worked with Campbell was back in '64. Only the wounded paid any mind to doctors, a fact Farley found utterly distasteful and completely unacceptable. And so he hatched a plan that he hoped would earn him the respect and admiration of his superiors...and more cash in his pay envelope as well.

General Bragg loved the ingenious idea so much that Farley was put in charge of the mission, from choosing the double agents with whom he worked to naming his own rank. Farley joined the Union army a lieutenant and left a corporal.

He trusted no one until they passed his acid test: enter a Confederate regiment as a buck private, and fight on the front lines alongside the Rebs—to the death, if necessary—against his own side to gain the trust of the enemy.

Only one man proved suitable, and much to his dismay, that man was seated at his table now, gorging himself with the supper Mrs. Farley had made that evening.

"I've been curious as a pup since your telegram arrived," Campbell said around a mouthful of corn bread. "When are you gonna tell me about this job you've lined up for me? No, wait," he said, using his fork as a pointer, "on second thought, before you answer, first tell me how much is in it for me." Chuckling, he peeled a hard-boiled egg. "No sense me being privy to any top secret information unless I'm agreeable to participating in the…ah…the covert operations."

"Five hundred dollars."

Campbell nodded thoughtfully. "Mmmmm…Well, now, that's a nice round number." He regarded him slyly. "If the likes of you thinks this job is worth a year's pay, it must be a filthy job, indeed. Filthy enough, I reckon, to bring a thousand."

Farley glowered. "Five hundred. Take it or leave it."

Campbell raised a hand in surrender. "Now, now, Doc. Don't get your neck hairs bristlin'. I might be persuaded to go under cover for that amount." He popped the egg into his mouth, whole, and washed it down with a swallow of whiskey. "Might, mind you," he said casually, buttering another slice of corn bread. "So, spill the beans, Doc. How am I to keep your so-called pacifist hands clean when the dirty deed gets done this time?"

Farley seated himself across from Campbell and folded both hands on the table. "I have found a way to aid in the postwar effort and boost my own income at the same time," he said, smirking as he fingered the curls of his handlebar mustache. "It involves plac-ing children orphaned by the war with farmers in the Midwest and beyond. There are a number of parentless children right here in town, and—"

Campbell just took a huge bite of ham. "Hold on there just a minute, Doc. You mean to say you've figured a way to kidnap young'uns made homeless by the war, and sell 'em like cattle?"

Haughtily, the doctor raised one brow. "Well, that's certainly putting it crudely, but…"

In an unguarded moment, the cynicism faded from Campbell's face and his near-black eyes glittered with disgust. The dark brows dipped low in the center of his forehead. "…but that's putting it accurately, am I right?"

Farley tightened his lips and leaned back in his chair. "You have always been astute, I'll give you that."

Campbell shot Farley a scathing, sideways look that silenced him. One side of his mouth raised in a near-snarl, he shoved his plate away. "You make me sick, Farley. I've done a heap of low-down things—some for pay, some just for the fun of it—but I've never harmed a young'un."

"Imagine," Farley all but sneered, "Hank Campbell, a man with a conscience." Shrugging, he nonchalantly tapped the edge of Campbell's plate. "If you haven't the stomach for the job, there are plenty of your kind out there who can do it." He grinned slightly.

"Without harming the young'uns?" He shrugged. "Who knows?"

Plates and eating utensils clattered to the floor as Campbell's huge hand shot out and grabbed a fistful of Farley's starched white shirt. He lifted Farley clean out of the chair and dragged him halfway across the table. "I'll do it," he bit out, "but only because the bank is about to foreclose on my ma and pa's farm."

He held Farley for a second, then two, and gave him a rough shove. The doctor landed so hard on the seat of his chair that a whoosh of air gushed from his lungs. In the moment it took to catch his breath, Farley cleared his throat and straightened his tie.

Campbell never took his eyes from Farley's as he drained the whiskey in his glass. "Any more where this came from?"

Wordlessly, the doctor went to the cupboard and retrieved the bottle as the hired gun ran a hand through his thick black hair and tilted his chair back on two legs. "Now, then," Campbell said, folding both hands over his food-stuffed yet flat belly, "what-say you tell me exactly how I'm supposed to help you get rich by takin' these poor young'uns."

Nate crooked an arm over his eyes and moaned softly in his sleep, hands tightfisted and stomach clenched as the dream sucked him deeper, deeper into the world of darkness. He tossed and turned, jaw clenched tight with agony as his subconscious mind struggled to stave off the ugly memories.

Despite his efforts, he slipped farther and farther from Ellicott City, and the here and now. Try as he might to cling to the present and protect himself from living it all over yet again, Nate remembered…

~

"Pass that bottle over here, you mangy polecat," grumped Mason. "We was lucky to get any whiskey at all, and there you sit, hoggin' it all to yourself."

Reluctantly, Nate handed the bottle to the man beside him, and did a quick mental head count…Mason, Campbell, and Powers would each take a swig…and it would be his turn again. Lying on his side near the campfire, he levered himself up on one elbow and bent one leg at the knee, trying to appear unconcerned as the men pressed the bottle to their lips, and exhaled satisfied "Ahhhs" before sending it on.

"Don't give it no never-mind if'n we drain this'n," Campbell said, eyes slanted in a grin, "there's more where that came from." His hand disappeared into his haversack, and reappeared wrapped around the neck of a full bottle of barley-bree.

Nate's mouth watered and his heart lurched at the sight of it. He already downed half a pint of the brew, and was beginning to feel its mind-numbing, dizzying effects. Warmed further by the steamy July night, he grinned at his comrade. "Well, then, what're you waitin' for, Campbell?" Nate leaned forward and extended his hand. "Let's have a taste of your new brew."

"Not so fast, O'Neil," the man laughed, clutching the bottle to his chest. "You're on guard duty tonight, aren't you?"

Disappointed at the reminder, he frowned slightly. "Aye, that I am. But another sip or two won't put me down."

From the corner of his eye, Campbell regarded him for a moment. "Well, all right then," he said, rolling the bottle to Nate, "I guess a swig or two won't hurt none."

The bottle collided into the sole of Nate's boot with a soft clink, sending the whiskey into a slip-sliding frenzy of sloshing waves that gleamed through the glass like sparkling honey. In seconds, he grabbed the bottle, uncorked it, and tilted it up to his lips.

"Whoa, there," Campbell said, chuckling. "I said you could have a swig or two...not drain the thing in one gulp!"

Begrudgingly, he handed it back to its rightful owner. "Where'd you get it?" Nate wanted to know, smacking his lips. "'Tis mighty hard to come by these days."

Campbell held the bottle to his own mouth. "You got that right! I had to trade my daddy's watch fob for it!" He passed the bottle to Nate.

They might have continued to pass it back and forth that way 'til dawn, if a bedraggled soldier hadn't stepped into the circle of men sitting around the campfire. "Get on over to your post, O'Neil. It's your turn up on Sanctuary Ridge."

Nate looked up into the haggard man's face. "Who's watchin' it now, while you're standin' here barkin' orders?"

"Nobody. All the more reason for you to hustle your sorry bones over there!"

Nate held the bottle out to Campbell. The man took it, and as he bent to tuck it into his bedroll, Nate gathered up his hat and his gun and headed for his post.

Halfway there, footsteps behind him made Nate stop in his tracks. "Wait up, O'Neil," came the coarse whisper.

It was Campbell, grinning as he sidled up beside him. "Here," he said, handing the bottle back to Nate. "She'll keep you company through this lonely night."

Nate looked longingly at the bottle. "No, I'd better not."

"Aw, go on," Campbell pressed. "I've been watchin' you for months now. Look at these drunken sots around you. They can't even stand up, and you're not even staggering. You know how to handle your liquor better'n most."

The light of the distant campfire shimmered on the whiskey's surface, like flecks of brassy starlight. Slowly, he eased his hand around the bottle's neck, then met Campbell's eyes. "Thanks, friend," he said, a half smile on his face. Hoisting the bottle as he headed for the ridge, a grin lit his eyes. "I'll raise her in a toast to you, my man, as I sit on the hard ground watchin' over your ornery sleepin' soul."

A good-natured salute was Campbell's only response. And ducking low, he headed back for his bedroll.

Nate sat alone in the dark, humming old ballads and hymns to pass the time until his relief showed up. After an hour or so, the tunes began to parch his throat, and he wet it with a generous swallow of Campbell's whiskey.

It took but a moment for a loud whirring sound to begin buzzing inside his head. Soon, his gut was whirling, too. Nate planted a boot flat on the ground to push himself up to a standing position; perhaps a bit of a walk would rouse him from the heavy, sleepy sounds bubbling in his ears.

But the foot slid, putting his leg straight out once more. *What's goin' on?* he wondered, palms pressed to his pounding temples. Dozens of times in the past weeks, he consumed three times this much whiskey, and never experienced anything even remotely like this!

He willed his eyes open, his head up. But try as he might, his body would not obey even the slightest command. And then his brain ceased giving commands. Nate slumped sideways, disappearing in a rounded-out crevice between the rocks. He was dead asleep before he hit bottom.

The pungent scent of charred wood roused him. Head aching with agonizing pain, he pressed his knuckles to his eyes, trying to identify the sounds of suffering filtering into his throbbing ears. Something dreadful happened…perhaps a fox invaded a raccoon's den to nab a kit for supper.

He patted the ground around him, thinking to find his rifle and head into the woods to hunt for the innocent kits. When he found them, he aimed his weapon and put them out of their misery.

The sky glowed the deep velvety purple that signals the approaching dawn. It took all the strength he could muster to lift himself into a sitting position. Then, with a great groan, he stood.

And the shock of what he saw nearly knocked him off his feet again.

All around him, death.

And beyond it, dying.

It hadn't been a nest of raccoon kits, mewling out after a fox attack. It was his fellow soldiers, helpless and moaning in their bedrolls. Scattered among the wounded, their motionless comrades did not whimper in pain.

As Nate slept, the Yankees invaded and slaughtered them where they laid.

Why didn't you hear anythin'? he demanded of no one. *Why not a shout or a cry, or even a gunshot?* Surely this much murder and mayhem had not taken place in stony silence!

Silent or not, the attack happened…on his watch.

On his watch!

Darting from one mutilated body to the next, Nate knelt and inspected each man's wound. Tamping down the guilt rising in him like bitter bile, he offered the barely living comfort and assurance. "Lie still now and fill your mind with thoughts of those you love, 'cause help is comin'."

But even as he spoke the words, he knew they were lies. Men not yet dead soon would be, Nate believed, unless they received immediate medical care. Eyes overflowing with tears of shame and anguish, he stood, intent upon heading north, where he knew a small battalion was positioned. Perhaps there would be a medic among them, and bandages, and morphine.

A searing pain shot through his upper chest, knocking him flat on his back. Lost in self-recrimination, Nate never saw the attack coming. As he lay there bleeding and staring into the brightening sky, he admitted a few things to himself: *The Yanks left a sniper or two behind to pick off the survivors, and one of 'em has taken me down.* He hoped the wound were mortal, for he certainly didn't feel he deserved to live when so many died because of his drunken stupor! With the pain of the gunshot and the pain of humiliation ringing in his ears, Nate succumbed to unconsciousness.

Nearly a day later, he woke in the infirmary unable to move, thanks to the stiff white bandage crossing from his chest to his left shoulder. "You certainly took your time comin' 'round, soldier," drawled the man standing over him. "I'm Doctor Wolffe."

You look more like a butcher than a doctor in that bloody apron, Nate told him silently, wincing as Wolffe's stethoscope pressed near the wound.

"We came close to diggin' a hole for your remains," Wolffe said, straightening, "but you fooled the Grim Reaper." Winking, he added, "You'll survive."

They should have been calming, reassuring words. Instead, they filled Nate with dread. Why had God allowed him to live after what he did? Nate turned his face away from the doctor. "How long 'til I'm out of this place?" he asked—his voice thick with grief and guilt.

"You'll be here a few days, perhaps a week. But a wound like that'll take a long time to heal."

Nate met Wolffe's eyes for the first time. "I've got to fight. The others...they...I...."

As the doctor turned and began examining the man on the next cot, he tossed over his shoulder: "I admire your courage and your fortitude, son, but your days of soldiering are over."

Courage! he thought, heart pounding with disbelief. Men died, dozens of them, because his cowardice drove him to drink when the pressures of battle grew too heavy to bear. "But, 'tisn't fair," he protested weakly. "It's me duty…the least I can do, considerin'.…"

"There's nothing fair about war, son."

True enough, Nate admitted, frowning inwardly. *How fair is it that you came through with barely a scratch and the others…?* The picture of oozing wounds and exposed bones of his fellow soldiers flashed through his mind. *You don't deserve to live, for you're a.…*

A blood-chilling bellow of pain sliced through the quiet tension in the tent and woke Nate from his nightmare.

He sat on the edge of the cot, head in his hands, shivering. A glance at the stove explained the chill in the room. Ordinarily, the crackling fire and radiant coals were easily visible through the thick black grating, low on the front of the stove. Not so this morning.

He was cold, so cold, as though a wintry snow fell during the night, covering him with an icy-white blanket.

With a heavy sigh, he stood and moved woodenly forward, drawn by the dim glow of the fire's dwindling embers. Mechanically, he wrapped his fingers around the poker's handle and stirred the crimson cinders in the stove's belly. Gently, he blew a puff of air across the bed of coals, bringing the fire gradually to life. Tiny flames, born of sparks, flared yellow and orange and red, burning hotter and brighter as Nate added kindling to the coals. "The fires of hell reserved for me," he ground out, his gaze settling on the floorboard that hid the bottle of whiskey, "because of you."

Overwhelmed by his years of guilt, he dropped to the floor and, with his bare hands, ripped the board up and threw it aside. As if it were a fussing infant, he gently lifted the bottle and cradled it to his chest, a thumb caressing its black and white label. Licking his lips, he uncorked it, brought it nearer, nearer his quivering lips.

Rage roiled inside him as the scent of whiskey wafted into his nostrils. Mouth drawn back in a fierce snarl, he whirled around and began pouring the liquor into the fire.

The flames flared brightly, threatening to envelop the hand that held the bottle. Startled by the sudden heat, Nate dropped the bottle into inferno, and within minutes, it exploded with a hollow pop, sending a spray of fiery shards showering around his feet.

And from the shadows, a deep voice said, "Seems like a waste of good whiskey to me."

FIVE

Startled by the deep voice, Nate lurched and searched the shadows for its owner. "What're you doin' here?" he rasped.

Leaning casually in the doorway, Hank Campbell inspected the bit of hay he'd been chewing, then slowly met Nate's eyes. Shrugging one shoulder. "Now, now, O'Neil," he smirked, "I'm sure your mama raised you better. Is that any way to greet a man who fought beside you against the Blue bellies?"

Running a hand through sleep-disheveled hair, Nate gathered his wits. "It's been a long time, Hank."

Nothing moved, save the narrowing of Campbell's dark eyes. "July 29, 1864; four months shy of two years."

In the past, when meeting up with an old chum, Nate found himself rushing forward and grabbing the man's hand and lifting his arm up and down like a pump handle in exuberant greeting. There was playful shoving and good-natured arm punching, and a hearty round of laughter as they went about the business of catching up.

There was no such warmth in this reunion.

"So," Nate said, feeling obliged to say something halfway companionable, at least, to this man who fought dozens of battles beside with him, "how are you?"

"Fine, fine. And you?"

"Can't complain."

Hank pocketed both hands, moved the straw to the other side of his mouth. Still slouching against the door frame, he regarded Nate through narrowed eyes. He nodded toward the broken glass scattered all around Nate's feet. "You seem a mite jittery." His smile never reached his eyes when he added, "I hope that wasn't your last bottle."

Something in the man's tone told Nate that Hank hadn't come here to exchange early-morning pleasantries. "Aye. 'Twas me last. But it's all right, 'cause I don't drink anymore." And before Campbell could respond, Nate quickly added, "What brings you to Maryland, Hank? Surely the weather's more pleasant in Tennessee this time of year."

Something akin to guilt flickered across Campbell's rugged face at the mention of his home state, and Nate wondered what could rouse such obvious discomfort in response to the simple question.

Campbell gave another shrug. "The war took its toll on the South, as I'm sure you know. Jobs are scarce and the women are scarcer still." Winking, he said, "I hear there's plenty of work—and women—to spare up here." He nodded toward the stairs, indicating the workshop below. "What line of work are you in these days, O'Neil?"

Nate explained that to meet the needs of friends and neighbors, he combined his talents and become part-blacksmith, part-carpenter, and part-wheelwright, building the shop single-handedly and modeling the turbine after one he operated in Ireland. "The townsfolk keep me workin' fairly steady."

The answer prompted an approving nod from Campbell. "Interesting. Maybe you could use an assistant."

That inspired a quiet chuckle. Nate shook his head. "'Fraid I can't help you, Hank. Most of my so-called customers are even poorer than me. Better'n half the time, they pay me with chickens and slabs of bacon." Almost as an afterthought, he said, "You're welcome to join me for breakfast. There's more'n an ample supply of ham and eggs."

At the mention of food, Campbell straightened and put his full weight on both feet. "Don't mind if I do." He draped an arm across Nate's shoulders as they headed for the squatty woodstove in the middle of the floor. "Maybe while we eat, you can tell me if you've heard of anyone else who might be hiring. I mean, that's the least you can do since..."

Every muscle in him tensed. Would Campbell say, *Since your drunkenness nearly put me into an early grave?*

"...since we're old army buddies and all," he finished, smirking.

From the moment he joined Nate's regimen in April of '64, Nate had Campbell pegged for a shrewd-minded sort, always looking for a good deal, a free ride, a get-rich-quick scheme. He was not the type to travel all the way from Tennessee to Maryland in the hopes of finding a job. *But what reason has he to lie?* Nate wondered. *And why is he here?*

He'd seen Campbell loading a buckboard in town. Why would the man buy flour and canned goods unless he already secured a place to store and cook them? And if he was looking for honest work because he was down on his luck, how had he paid for those supplies? *Well, the man's here now,* he thought, grabbing the big iron skillet from the peg above the stove, *and there's nothin' to do but deal with that.* If Campbell truly was as hungry as he claimed— and Nate suspected even that was a lie—perhaps a full belly and a grateful spirit would loosen his tongue.

⌒

Matt was in town, delivering packages for the widow Henderson when he stumbled over a small girl, huddled in the alley off Main Street. Groceries scattered and his hat flew off when he hit the ground with a quiet oomph. "What kind of person sits on the ground with both legs poking out to trip folks?" he demanded, jamming his wide-brimmed hat back onto his head. Crawling around to stuff the fallen groceries back into their box, he sat back on his heels. "I've never seen you before. What're you doing here?"

"I could ask the same question," the girl said, nervously fidgeting with one dark braid.

Matt stood and regarded her carefully. "I'm working," he snapped, "and this is a shortcut. But I asked you first."

Tears welled in her eyes. "I...I was only going to sit down for a minute to catch my breath," she began. "I got off the train and... and I was running and running, and..."

Wincing, Matt thumped his forehead with the heel of his palm. "Hey," he complained, "don't cry. It's okay. You don't have to explain."

Suddenly, his blue eyes widened and he held a forefinger in the air. "Say! Wait a minute...did you say you came to town on the train?"

The little brunette nodded.

"To meet Doctor Aubrey Farley?"

Her mouth dropped open in surprise. "How did you know?"

Narrowing one eye, Matt scratched his chin. "Seems to me there's something funny going on here. First Curtis, and now you."

"Who's Curtis?" she said, scrambling to her feet.

"He got off the train to meet Farley a couple months back. Took one look at the mean old buzzard and took off for parts unknown." Matt grinned. "And ran into me."

She only sighed.

"Curtis came from Richmond. Where did you get on the train?"

"Charlotte."

"Curtis is an orphan. His whole family got killed in the war."

Tears welled in her brown eyes again. "M-m-mine, too."

"It's all right," he interrupted, a hand on her shoulder. "Don't talk about it anymore." He gave her a quick once-over. "Is that the only dress you have?"

She pointed at the small satchel at her feet. "There's another one in there. And a pair of wool stockings, and new shoes, too."

Matt peeked into the bag. "New? These things are hand-me-downs twice over! Where'd you get 'em?"

She bit her trembling lip. "The church ladies gave them to me. I was to wear them to meet…my new…my…" A sob choked off her words.

Matt hoisted the box in one arm. "When was the last time you had anything to eat?" he wanted to know, his free hand tugging her from the alley.

"Last night they gave us a cheese sandwich on the train."

"They?"

"The ladies from the Children's Aid Society."

"A cheese sandwich! That's all?" He shook his head and scowled.

"And a cup of water."

His scowl deepened. "And they call themselves Christians." Matt gave her another inspection. "Well, I suppose you're not starving to death or anything, but you sure could use some meat on those bones."

The girl let him pull her along beside him.

"Soon as I take these groceries over to Mrs. Houghton's house, I'll bring you home. Emma will fix you right up."

"Emma?"

"She's my new mother."

"You're…you're an orphan, too?"

"Yup. Nearly eight months now." He clenched his jaw and swallowed to control the sob that rose up at every mention of his past. "Don't you worry," he told his small companion. "Emma will take care of you, too."

"But...but won't she be angry if you bring home a...?"

Chuckling, Matt headed across the street. "We have a cat and a dog, and a one-legged robin at our house," he said, grinning proudly, "and I found each and every one of them in the woods... same place I met up with Curtis. She never even batted an eye when I brought 'em home."

Again, silence was her response. And after awhile, she said, "You're very big. How old are you?"

"Nearly eleven. You?"

"Ten." Her dark brows furrowed slightly.

"Ten! But you're such a teeny little thing."

"And you're as big as any man I've seen. How'd you get so huge in just ten years?"

"Ten and a half," Matt smiled and shrugged. "Take after my pa, I guess. He was tall as a tree and big around as a bear. Strong, too," he added, lifting the box up and down to prove he inherited his father's might. And when she blinked admiringly up at him, he smiled wider.

"So, do you have a name, or should I call you Pipsqueak?"

Grinning, she said, "I'm Marcie. Marcie Miller." Looking up into Matt's eyes, she added, "But you can call me Pipsqueak if you want to."

They strolled along in silence for a moment or two before Marcie said, "There are others, you know."

He stopped walking and faced her. "What do you mean 'others'?"

"Other children who got off the train to meet Dr. Farley."

He glanced over his shoulder. "You mean, back there, in the alley?"

Marcie nodded. "A boy named Ryan, and his little brother and sister."

"None of you went with Farley?"

She shook her head. "It was Ryan's idea to hide. He said he heard the other children talking on the train. Some of them said he isn't really a doctor; he's a cannibal and he eats children for supper."

"Well, that's just ridicu—"

"...and some," she continued, mindless of Matt's interruption, "said he kidnaps children, and sells them as slaves to rich farmers out west. Ryan says either way, Dr. Farley looks mean as a snake. He was afraid you might tell on us." She stared at the toes of her grimy boots. "I didn't move fast enough. That's why you tripped over me."

"So...where is this Ryan person, anyway?"

"When he heard you coming, he hid behind the trash bins in the alley. But he wouldn't have," she added, smiling sweetly, "if he'd known you were so nice."

Matt mirrored her smile, then sighed. "Where did you think you were going once Farley realized there was nobody meeting him on that train?"

Marcie frowned. "I...I don't think Ryan had a plan." She sighed again. "I know I didn't."

"Well, we can't leave them in the alley, that's for sure. It's gonna get good and cold once the sun goes down." He stood for a moment, as if debating whether to do his job or see to the children first. "I have an idea," he said, leaning his palms on his knees to put himself eye to eye with Marcie. "You go back there and wait for me. It'll take fifteen or twenty minutes to finish up at the store, and then we'll head straight over to Emma's."

He didn't wait for her to agree to do as he suggested. Instead, Matt darted out into the street and headed for Mrs. Henderson's house. Minutes later, he was handing over the rumpled groceries.

"Where are you off to in such an all-fired hurry?" the widow asked when he headed for the door.

"Gotta get some more orphans over to Emma's," he hollered over his shoulder. "See you after school tomorrow!"

Any other day, it would have taken ten minutes to get from the general store to the alley up the street. Today, Matt covered the distance in five. And if he hadn't already been winded when he rounded the corner, Matt suspected he'd have grown breathless by his first sight:

Marcie stood in the middle, bundling a tiny baby in her arms. To her left, a boy no more than five, and to her right, a boy of perhaps twelve. Their faces were dirty and streaked with the tracings of dried tears, their clothes even shabbier than Marcie's. "How long have you been here?" Matt asked, stepping farther into the alley.

"Since last night," Marcie answered, "I told you...."

He looked around the dark, dingy alley. "You spent the whole night here? Alone?" His gaze settled on the baby she held. "Even that?"

Marcie quirked a brow. "Not that," she corrected. "She. Her name is Becky." She tucked the filthy blanket around the baby's face. "She's hungry, but we don't have any milk."

"No money to buy it, either. And even if we did, we ain't got no bottle to put it in," Ryan injected.

Ain't got no! Matt repeated silently. Later, Emma would teach Ryan about the word "ain't" and the use of double negatives. Right now, these children needed care and attention.

"C'mon," Matt said, lifting the little boy in his arms. "We're going to Emma's house."

"Emma?" the child echoed.

"That's right," Matt said as he walked. "What's your name?" Grinning mischievously, the boy grabbed Matt's nose and pinched with all his might.

"Ow!" Matt yelled. "I said 'name', not 'nose'!"

Giggling, Marcie fell into step beside him. "His name is Steven." She nodded to Steven's older brother. "And that's Ryan." Rubbing her nose against the baby's, she added, "Isn't Becky adorable?"

He gave the baby a cursory glance. To Matt, she looked like a little pink tomato worm. "Yeah. Adorable." Then, "There's Emma's house up there," he announced, pointing.

The children climbed the steps and waited as Matt pushed open the door. "Emma," he called. "Emma...we're home."

She had barely reacted when he came in with Curtis. So why did she gasp as if she'd just stepped on a snake? And why was she just standing there, hands over her mouth and blue eyes wide as saucers?

Much as she loved him, Emma knew she needed to have a little talk with Matt regarding the way he brought her all manner of strays. *It's like a game to you, Matt,* she thought, *but it's no game. If we're going to have all these children, we need to be able to feed and clothe them!*

A bath, clean clothes, and a hot meal were exactly what the doctor ordered for Marcie, Ryan, and Steven, but the baby was another matter entirely.

Her nurse's training quickly made Emma realize the child suffered from consumption. If little Becky was to survive the horrible coughing spasms and the high fever, she'd need round-the-clock attention. *How will I work for Farley at the clinic and take care of these poor children...one of them deathly ill?* she worried, pacing the darkened parlor. *If you can't work, you can't buy food. And without food, they'll be almost as bad off as before you took them in!*

In the note she'd received from Brother Aphrates yesterday, he wrote that Curtis could meet the Joneses at Emma's house, day after tomorrow. He seemed like a man who had his fingers on the pulse of the town; perhaps the good brother knew of other families who could take in a child...or three.

She slumped wearily into the rocker near the hearth and kissed the baby's fever-hot forehead. "I'll discuss it with him first thing in the morning," she whispered into Becky's warm little ear.

Between coughing fits—which came at nearly hourly intervals—the infant snuggled close and slept in Emma's arms. The sound of Emma's soft voice seemed to soothe and calm the fretful child, and so she sang every song she knew in a quiet, loving voice. Now and then, Emma dozed as she patted the baby's tiny back. Mostly, she stared into space and wondered how on earth she was going to see to the needs of seven children.

Dear Lord, she prayed, *show me Your bountiful peace.*

And the verses she memorized as a girl from the Book of Luke came to mind.

"*...consider the ravens: for they neither sow nor reap; which neither have storehouse nor barn; and God feedeth them: how much more are ye better than the fowls?...consider the lilies how they grow: they toil not, they spin not; and yet I say unto you, that Solomon in all his glory was not arrayed like one of these. If then God so clothed the grass, which is to day in the field, and tomorrow is cast into the oven; how much more will he clothe you, O ye of little faith? Seek not what ye shall eat, or what ye shall drink, neither be ye of doubtful mind...your Father knoweth that ye have need of these things...*"

Emma breathed a sigh of relief. Smiling, she slipped into a peaceful slumber, and dreamt of a table, draped in a white cloth and covered with food enough for her orphans.

⌒

"And the way I figure it, me and Ryan, here, can help you build things to earn some extra money. He's not as big as me, but he was raised on a farm. I'm sure he's a good hard worker..."

"Matthew," Nate started, arms raised in a helpless gesture, "much as I'd like to help you and your friends, I'm afraid there's not enough work these days to keep me in rice and beans."

"But folks are always askin' you to fix things and build things."

"Aye," Nate said, laying his drill aside to put his hand on Matt's shoulder. "But most of 'em don't have any more money than you do." He pointed toward the work table. "See that pile of papers on the stickpin there?"

Matt nodded.

"They're lists of what the townsfolk owe me."

Frowning, Matt spat out, "Well, why don't you make 'em pay, then?"

Affectionately, he roughed up the boy's hair. "They'll pay when they can, and 'til they do, I'm keepin' track at their request."

Pouting, Matt shook his head. "My pa used to say a man has to pay his own way in this world; man can't expect a handout, so he has to work hard."

"Aye, there's truth in your da's words, Matthew. But times are hard since the war. Folks lost their farms, their businesses, their homes. If they had the money, I'm sure they'd be payin' what they owe." Nate chucked the boy under the chin. "There's wood for the fire and a roof over me head, and when they can, me customers bring a fat hen or a tin of biscuits around to fill me belly. I ain't in any hurry to be paid."

Matt headed for the door. "If people paid what they owed, then could I have a job?"

Nate followed him, then blocked his exit. "The minute I can afford an apprentice, you'll be my first choice," he said, smiling. "Now why don't you tell me what's really eatin' at you? It ain't the job, 'cause you know as well as I that dear Emma won't let those little ones starve."

"Oh, she'll feed 'em, all right," he snapped, "'til she can get rid of 'em."

Nate studied the boy's face. "Get rid of 'em? Whatever are you talkin' about, son?"

Stomping deeper into the workshop, Matt flopped onto a hay bale and crossed both arms over his chest. "She's giving Curtis away...to a family south of town. They're going to adopt him."

Down on one knee, he put his hand on the boy's arm. He'd seen Emma with Curtis; if she didn't love him with every fiber in her being, she was a fine actress, indeed. So fine that she ought to be performing with the Shakespearean company that toured from town to town. Nate couldn't imagine Emma giving Curtis up. "How d'you know this, Matthew?"

"Mr. and Mrs. Jones came by yesterday. They're Negroes, too, see, and Emma says they can't have any children of their own. She says they have a nice house and a good business in Elk Ridge and the school there is a fine one."

Picking at the straw beside his thigh, Matt sighed heavily. "They sat in the kitchen with Curtis for over an hour, talking. I heard Mr. Jones tell him he would never take a strap to his bee-hind." Sitting taller, Matt said in as deep a voice as he could muster: "'If you get out of line, I'll give you a dandy lecture, but I don't think that'll happen often, since you seem to be a well-behaved child.'"

He blinked and frowned and bit his bottom lip, struggling not to cry. "And when they left, Curtis went with them. Emma said he'd be better off with the Joneses, 'cause he'd have two loving parents, and cousins, and aunts, and uncles."

Nate raised a brow. "Did they drag him off, kickin' and screamin'?"

"No. He looked right glad to be going, which is a puzzle. He liked it at Emma's." He rolled his eyes. "She says he'll be even happier with the Joneses."

"Did you ever stop to think maybe she's right?" Nate asked softly.

Matt nodded. "But I didn't want him to go!"

"Aye, I understand somethin' about that. Ian and me, we're like this," Nate said, clasping his hands tight. "He's more'n my brother…he's my best friend, an' I love him with all my heart. It's natural that you love Curtis, and want to keep him close."

Matt's blue eyes flashed with fear and fury when he said, "If she loved him, how could she let him go? And how long 'til she palms me off on some family, sayin' it's for my own good!"

Ah, so that's it. The boy thinks it's just a matter of time 'til Emma puts him out, like a stray cat. He stood and began to pace, each booted footfall thumping on the pine board floor. Stroking his heard, he searched for the words Matt needed to hear. It struck like a thunderbolt: The boy needed nothing but the truth.

"Matthew," he said, perching on the corner of his work table, "did you ever hear about the woman whose child died in the night?"

Shaking his head, the boy met Nate's eyes.

"It's a Bible story from First Kings, y'see. Seems the woman was a guest in another woman's house. The owner of the house just had a baby of her own, don't y'know, so when the visitor's newborn died, she waited 'til her friend was asleep...and switched babies."

Matt gasped.

"The real mother claimed the live one as her own," Nate continued. "Started all manner of fuss an' bother, 'cause a mother knows her own wee one..."

"How did she know it was hers?"

"Her heart told her. Well, the bickerin' must have gone on for quite some time, 'cause eventually the pair of 'em ended up in the castle of old King Solomon. Him bein' the wisest feller in the land and all, I s'pose the real mother figured he'd see to it that she got her baby back, safe and sound."

"And did he? Did King Solomon give the lady's baby back?"

"Eventually...but how d'you think he did the job?"

"If he was the smartest man in the land, he could tell which woman was lying and...."

"Aye, it would seem just that simple, now wouldn't it? But smart as he was, Solomon wasn't God. He couldn't know for certain which was the real mother...especially with the both of 'em standin' there bawlin' like heifer calves and claimin' to be the baby's ma...."

Squinting one eye as he held a forefinger aloft, Nate said, "So old Solomon had himself a dandy idea. 'Bring me a sword!' he ordered. And a servant brought out the biggest, sharpest sword either woman had ever seen. 'What do you mean to do with that?' the pair of 'em wanted to know. 'Why, I'm going to cut the boy in half,' said Solomon, 'and give each of you an equal portion, that's what, and put a stop to this frettin' and fightin', once and for all.'"

Nate leapt to his feet and mimicked King Solomon. "Can you picture it, Matthew? Solomon, standin' there, that big sword high above his head, sayin, 'Put the babe on the table, so's I can split him in two!'"

Matt leaned forward. "And what happened then? Surely he didn't..." Swallowing, he shook his head. "Solomon didn't really cut the baby in..."

"Didn't have to," Nate said, winking. "When the true mother saw what he was about to do, she lay her body over the baby and cried out, '*Don't kill him, sir...she can have the baby if it means that much to her; just let him live!*' That's how Solomon knew which was the liar. He took that baby from the visitor and gave him to his real mother."

Smiling, Matt heaved a sigh of relief. Suddenly, he frowned. "But what does that have to do with Emma giving Curtis away?"

"Matthew, Matthew, Matthew," Nate said, raking a hand through his hair. "Don't you see? The real mother was willing to make a great sacrifice for her child. She loved him enough to let him go, to let another woman raise him, because that's what was best for her boy."

Comprehension flickered in Matt's eyes, and after a moment of mulling it over in his mind, he hung his head. "So maybe you're right. Maybe Curtis is better off living with the Joneses." He met Nate's eyes to add, "But I ain't Curtis, and I don't want to leave Emma, ever."

Kneeling, Nate plopped his hands on the boy's shoulders. "The woman loves you like her own flesh and blood, Matthew. You can be sure she'll only do what's best for you." He shrugged one shoulder. "If that's another family, you can be just as sure it'll be a good one. And if stayin' put is what's best for you in her mind, then I expect you'll be livin' in her house 'til you take yourself a bride."

"A bride!" Matt sputtered, wrinkling his nose. "I'm never getting married. Girls are…." He curled his lips and shuddered. "I'll never take a bride!"

Laughing, Nate stood and guided Matt to the door. "You're not feelin' any different right now than any other boy your age, Matthew, but I can tell you this: One day, you're gonna remember what you said here today, and you'll ask yourself whatever caused such blarney to squeak into your head." Nate pictured Emma's golden hair and clear blue eyes, and smiled fondly. "One day, you'll meet a fine, lovely young woman…"

Matt's nose crinkled in a grimace. "Yuck!"

Nate ignored the interruption. "…with a heart of gold and a gift for makin' folks feel—"

"Like Emma makes folks feel?"

Nate stopped dead in his tracks, heart beating double-time at the mere mention of her name.

"Do you like her, Nate?"

His chest swelled with the huge gulp of air he swallowed. "Aye," he admitted slowly. "That I do."

Matt shrugged. "Then why don't you ask her to be your bride?"

He met the boy's eyes, expecting to find a teasing glint glittering there. Instead, Nate saw that the boy's question had been posed for serious consideration. It was a question Nate had asked himself, dozens of times since that afternoon in her dining room. And the answer was always the same: "I'm afraid our darlin' Emma deserves a better husband than the likes of me, Matthew," he said in a raspy whisper.

And before the boy could voice the protest written all over his face, Nate pulled a coin from his pocket and pressed it into Matt's hand, and gave him a gentle shove. "Go on down to the store an' buy yourself some sweet treats," he called after the happily grinning boy. "Be sure get enough to share with the others, mind you!"

In moments, he was out of sight, yet Nate stood in the door, staring after him. "Ask Emma to be your bride," he repeated under his breath. Turning slowly, he trudged heavily into his workshop. "If the day ever dawned when I could do such a thing, I'd know God had smiled upon my soul."

So lost in thought was he that Nate never noticed the huge dark figure of a man, lurking in the shadows.

SIX

Leaning back in his chair, he stretched languidly. "Why, it'll be like the Pied Piper, leading them wherever we want them to go."

Farley regarded Campbell through hooded eyes. "I don't know," he said, stroking his handlebar mustache. "I just don't know."

Campbell put all four chair legs back on the floor and met the doctor's eyes. "It was a stroke of luck, I tell you, that he's the one."

The doctor crossed both arms over his chest. "From the moment I met him, I wondered why Nate O'Neil behaved like the walking wounded. But finding out why he's riddled with guilt and grief does us no good."

"For such a smart fellow," Campbell ground out, "you're as dumb as a post." He began counting on his fingers. "His whole family lives in this town. He's crazy about those young'uns. And he's got it bad for pretty Emma Wright. Every last one of 'em thinks the world of him, and he likes it that way."

Farley continued to stare from beneath puzzle-frazzled bushy brows. "I still fail to see how he could be of any use to us."

Exhaling a breath of vexation, Campbell ran both hands through his hair. "Don't you get it, Doc? All I have to do is suggest that I might blow the whistle on him, and he'll dance to our tune." Shrugging, he chuckled. "He doesn't want his family and the townsfolk knowing he had a part in killing nearly a hundred innocent men on the battlefield. They all think he's a war hero, for the luvva Pete, and he wants 'em to go right on believing that!"

One gray-white brow rose high on Farley's forehead as he considered Campbell's explanation. "I must admit, the fact that he was the man who made the Yankee attack possible that night is an incredible coincidence. But what possible use can we make of him this time?"

Campbell scrubbed both hands over his face. "I have a good mind to tack an extra hundred to your bill. I feel like a buttoned-up schoolmarm, having to hold your slimy hand and walk you through this job! Pay attention, why don't you, and take a look at what's right under your nose!

"O'Neil's sad-eyed conduct has endeared him to the good people of Ellicott City. And those orphans are particularly fond of him. I'd be willing to wager all five hundred dollars you're paying me that if he asked those young'uns to take a trip with him, they'd pack their bags that quick!" Campbell said, snapping his fingers for effect.

Farley tossed back a jigger of whiskey. He shook his head. "I say your plan is foolhardy, at best. My way might not be as gentle for the tenderhearted likes of you, but—"

"I'll show you tenderhearted!" Campbell stood so quickly, the chair clattered to the floor behind him. He stood, fists clenched at his sides and glared at Farley. "You hired me to do a job, and like it or not, I agreed to do it." He planted both meaty palms on the table and leaned in close. "But this is the way it's gonna be from here on out: either we do it my way, or I'm off the payroll."

He gave his threat a moment to penetrate Farley's brain, then said through clenched teeth. "Way I see it, you'll be months finding another hired gun. Besides, what you really need is a brain, since you're in short supply. By the time my replacement rolls into town—provided you can find one—opportunity may just have passed you by. Time's a-wastin', Doc. The war created a lot of orphans, but the war's over...and you ain't the only lowlife trying to make hay out of the misfortune of these young'uns."

Farley's lips narrowed as he sat looking into Campbell's dark, angry eyes.

"It's your choice, Doc. No skin off my nose either way. I'll find another way to help my ma and pa." He pushed himself to a standing position and grabbed his floppy-brimmed deerskin hat from the peg near the door. "When you've made up your mind," he said, settling it on his head, "you can find me at the saloon."

Aubrey Farley was many things, but a fool was not among them. He stared at the door Campbell deliberately left ajar, unconsciously rubbing his mustache as he considered all the man said. *He's right about one thing,* the doctor told himself, pouring another jigger of whiskey, *there isn't time to find a replacement.*

He downed the contents of the shot glass in one swallow, wincing as it slithered toward his gut in a searing trail. Rising slowly, he neatly pushed his chair under the table, smiling ruefully as he admitted Campbell's finesse. *He said you have two choices, but he knew full well he only left you with just one.*

Farley put on his hat and closed the door quietly behind him. As he headed for the saloon, where he'd agree to Campbell's terms, he popped a piece of licorice into his mouth. *Can't have the good folks of Ellicott City smelling liquor on your breath, now can we, Doctor Farley?*

⌒

My dear Mr. O'Neil,

I'm writing to thank you for the candy. It was a delightful treat. How kind of you to surprise the children this way!

Please allow us to show our thanks by joining us for dinner, immediately following Sunday services. (Matt will deliver your answer.)

Hoping to see you soon, I remain,

Gratefully yours,
Emma Wright

Nate read the note, then tucked it into his shirt pocket. "I'm not sure I can share another dinner with the bunch of you," he told Matt. "With so many mouths to feed, and what with the littlest one keepin' Emma from collectin' any pay..." He frowned. "It'd be like takin' food from the mouths of babes!"

Matt tucked in one corner of his mouth. "So, I'm to tell her you don't want to have dinner with us?"

"'Tisn't that I don't want to, Matthew. Why, I'd like nothin' better than to take another meal with—" *with that lovely woman,* he thought—"with the lot of you. But my conscience would nag me hard if I did."

The boy sighed. "Let me get this straight," he said, hands up as in surrender. "So I'm to tell Emma you want to come to dinner, only you can't."

Disappointment furrowed Nate's brow. "That pretty well says it, doesn't it?"

"She's going to want to know why."

It was Nate's turn to sigh. "Well, truth be, I have orders to fill. There's the water trough for Bud Stern and the cradle for me brother's wife, and the new desk for the schoolhouse."

Matt headed for the door. "Alright. I'll tell her you're too busy. But I know what she's going to say."

Nate raised a brow as he waited for the boy's prediction. "She'll send me right back here to invite you for next Sunday." Combing his fingertips through his beard, Nate nodded.

"Aye, that'd be like her, all right."

Just then, the hens penned in the corner of the workshop kicked up a fuss, cackling and clucking and fluttering their wings. A smile lit his eyes. "I have a splendid idea, Matthew, but you'll have to spend an hour or so here with me to make it work."

"Why?"

"See that stack of wood over there?" he asked, pointing to the tidy pile of lumber near the far wall.

Matt nodded.

"Well, you're goin' to move it..." he looked left, then right, and when his gaze settled on a spot near the door, he said, "...there."

"But..."

"Now, I haven't the money to pay you for your help, mind you, so I'm afraid you'll have to settle for..."

"Chickens!" Matt shouted, grinning with delight. "What a good idea. Emma won't be embarrassed because she doesn't have enough food to feed you, and you won't be embarrassed to eat what little she has!"

Matt ran over to the lumber pile and lifted the first board. Laying it near the door, he said, "But you're not fooling me, Nate. I don't think this wood really needs to be moved."

"What're you talkin' about, son? I got a hankerin' to see some change in my life, 'tis all."

"Change?"

"To see the placement of that pile of wood changed..."

"...From here, to there," Matt said, and pointed along with Nate. "I think you're just having me move it to give you an excuse to send me home with the chickens."

Nate regarded the boy a silent moment before a half grin slanted his thick mustache. "You're a smart boy, I'll give you that. You could be right," he shrugged nonchalantly, giving the wheel several hard cranks, "but you'll never know for sure." He watched water fill the turbine. "'Cause the sound of my saw, gnawing through these boards will drown out the admission...or denial...."

❧

As he scoured the woods for suitable trees to fell, Nate found a patch of wild jonquils growing on the banks of the Patapsco. He plucked a dozen or so from their pine needle beds. *Tomorrow,* he told himself, *Emma will have flowers.*

Their golden petals glowed like velvety sunshine, despite the gray day, stirring a smile inside him, and the smile inspired a poem to take shape in his mind, a poem he recited aloud as he headed back to his shop.

She'll have flowers on the morrow,
 and she'll hold them near her heart.
Her eyes will mist and she will sigh,
 "You and I will never part."
Then she'll take my hand and lead me
 to the ocean's pounding shore, and look
 into my eyes to say, "I'll love you evermore."
She'll press a kiss upon me lips,
 and with breath that's whisper-sweet,
 she'll tell me I'm the darlin' man
 who's made her life complete.
Oh, my heart will start to poundin'
 and my soul will soar on high,
 for she's the lass God chose to live a lifetime at my side.
Then I'll take her in my grateful arms,
 and hold her ever-tight, for I cannot let this
 lovely lass go an arm's length from me sight.
"You'll have flowers when you're walkin',
 you'll have flowers when you ride.
 I'll fill your life with blooms!" I'll say,
 if you'll just be me bride."
And she'll toss those flowers out to sea,
 and watch them float away.

"It's you I need, not flowers," she'll say,
    "forever and a day."
Then she'll take my hand and lead me
    from the ocean's pounding shore,
    and look into my eyes to say,
    "I'll love you evermore."
Yes, she'll have flowers on the morrow,
    and she'll hold them near her heart,
    whilst I pray to God in heaven above,
"Please don't ever let us part."

He tried valiantly to busy himself through the remainder of the day, putting the lumber Matt stacked back where it was in the first place, rearranging cans of paint and bottles of turpentine on the shelves behind his worktable, pre-drilling holes in boards that he'd someday fashion into sleds or tubs or wagon beds.

Like the child who burrows deep into his covers an hour before bedtime, thinking the sooner to sleep, the sooner St. Nick would arrive, Nate retired earlier than usual. In place of sugarplums, thoughts of Emma danced in his head. Pictures of her floated behind tight-closed lids, the sound of her musical voice echoed in his ears.

When at last the sun squeaked over the horizon and lit the small space he called home, Nate all but leapt from his cot. Before retiring, he'd washed and pressed his best white shirt...the one with the balloon sleeves and embroidered pocket Mary had made him for Christmas last year. He owned two pair of trousers, sturdy cotton for work, and gabardine that he saved for funerals and weddings. He'd wear the good ones today with the fancy shirt, and string Ian's tie around his neck, as well!

When at last Nate stepped onto her porch, he peered at his reflection in the door's etched-glass window. Smoothing a wayward lock of dark hair into place, he rapped lightly on the glass.

He thought he knew how she'd react when that door swung open in welcome. At first sight of the flowers, her eyes would light up like the blue flames that burned hot and bright in the belly of his forge. She'd clasp those strong-yet-delicate hands beneath her chin and smile in that warm, womanly way of hers, then focus so completely on him that he'd likely forget to hand her the jonquils.

Nate was forced to mask his disappointment when Jenni answered his knock in Emma's stead. "Mr. O'Neil," the girl said, smiling. "Won't you come in?" She took his jacket and hung it on the hall tree. "Might I bring you a cup of tea? Emma just brewed a pot."

His gaze shot up the hall, searching for Emma, but he quickly returned his attention to the girl. "I'd like that," he said a bit absently.

"One lump or two?"

He pocketed both hands and shook his head. "Bein' around your sweetness is sugar enough for me," he said, smiling, "but I wouldn't mind a dollop of milk, if you have any to spare."

Blushing at the compliment, Jenni lifted her skirts and dashed into the kitchen. "Make yourself at home in the parlor," she called over her shoulder. "I'll tell Emma you're here."

Standing at the end of the sofa nearest the fireplace, Nate basked in the warmth of Emma's home. The crisp, clean scent of beeswax buzzed in the air, telling him she recently polished the furniture. One fat, fringed pillow nestled in each blue wing-backed chair, and a small footstool, upholstered in sea green damask to match the sofa, sat between them on the blood-red Persian rug. On the stool perched a basket of yarn, knitting needles, and cro-chet hooks.

He was in this parlor eight months ago, mere days after arriv-ing in Ellicott City. It was a late August day when he and Ian drove past Stella's house on their way into town. Ian told Nate about the woman who was the first to extend the warm hand of friendship when the O'Neils first came to town. She was dying, Nate's brother had said, and so was the once-beautiful old house she lived in.

Her niece, Ian said, was holding her own with the small jobs out of town. But the last thunderstorm blew several tiles from her roof and cracked a pane of glass in the parlor window...jobs that required a man's strong hand. Ian did what he could for Stella, but with the business to run and a family to care for, there wasn't time for every repair.

But Nate had time, every moment of every hour, it seemed, filled with dreaded thoughts of that night on the battlefield. Long hard days, he found, helped block some of the bitter memories.

And so he took it upon himself to help the poor dying spinster woman who'd helped his family. Ian had mentioned a niece, and Stella confirmed it. They said her name was Emma, and that she'd become Dr. Farley's nurse, just as soon as she returned from Baltimore; if another female lived in the house, she obviously inherited her aunt's dark, over-decorated style.

Now, he pocketed both hands and paced the parlor floor. It was a gloomy room when he replaced that broken pane of glass, with burgundy walls trimmed in deep blue, done up in the fussy style of the day, from the gaudy lamps to the scattered bric-a-brac.

Hands clasped at his lower back, Nate prowled about, nodding approvingly at the changes Emma made. The overpowering walls were creamy white now, the trim boards pale yellow. She'd taken down the heavy velvet draperies and replaced them with gauzy white curtains. The knickknacks were tucked into one curved curio cabinet, and the garish red-fringed trim on the lantern shades was gone.

She turned the parlor into a bright-yet-calm space any man would feel at home in, with no fear of mussing the ruffles and frills that, in his mind, made a house look feminine and overdone.

He found it odd there were no lithographs anywhere in the room...not even one of her dear departed auntie Nate saw quite a few that day when he stopped by to repair the broken window seat. He remembered one in particular, Stella on the sofa, smiling proudly, one arm around a very young, very pretty Emma. And one where Emma posed alone, fingers splayed on the keys of the parlor piano. There were dozens of silver- and brass-framed camera portraits lining the mantle. *Where were they now?* he wondered.

Jenni stepped slowly into the room, frowning with concentration as she balanced the tea service on a carved wood tray. She sighed with relief once the tray was safe on the table. "Emma says to tell you she'll be down in a minute." Straightening, Jenni grinned and chanced a glance at the door. "She's been changing outfits and re-doing her hair all morning," she whispered, "which is silly, since she had to get dressed for Sunday services." Hiding a giggle behind a dainty hand, the girl added, "People are going to get the impression she's sweet on you, Mr. O'Neil!"

He smiled and sat on the sofa. "I'd be honored if a woman like Emma was…"

"…If a woman like Emma was what?"

Nate got slowly to his feet, and found himself unable to speak, for Emma breezed into the room looking like an angel in her pale pink dress, her hair spilling down her back like liquid sunshine. Up to this point, he always saw her in sensible skirts made of dark, durable materials, and plain high-button blouses, and she always wore her hair in a no-nonsense bun. Despite the practical outfits—or maybe because of them—he thought her a rare beauty. But beautiful seemed a terribly inadequate word to describe the way she looked today.

He could only hope she would not repeat her question, for if she did, he couldn't very well say, "I'd be honored—no—delighted to learn that a woman like Emma Wright is sweet on me," now could he! Fortunately, she cradled an infant in her arms, and the child seemed to have taken every bit of her attention.

Emma marched right up to him. "Nate," she said, gently kissing the baby's forehead, "I'd like you to meet Rebecca Donnelly." Smiling, she met his eyes to add, "We call her Becky."

He wrapped his big hand around the baby's fragile fingers and gave a gentle "how-do" shake. "Pleased to meet you, beautiful Becky."

Emma turned slightly and faced the door. "Come, come." she instructed lightly, waving three more children into the room, "I want you to meet a dear friend of mine."

Nate's heart lurched when she called him "friend." *I'd much prefer the title "husband,"* he thought wryly, *but since that can never be, I suppose I'll settle for "friend."*

"This is Ryan, and this is Steven. They're Becky's big brothers. And this," she said, one hand on a dark-haired girl's arm, "is Marcie."

The way the children stood, stiff-backed and grim-faced, made Nate's heart ache. He wondered how these youngsters came to be parentless, and how they ended up in Emma's care. But there was time for that later. For now, they needed nothing more than to hear that he would gladly be their friend, too.

"'Tis a pleasure to know you," he said, smiling as he shook each child's hand. "How long have you been in town?"

"Two weeks," Ryan answered. He glanced at Matt, who stood nearby, grinning. "He found us in an alley, and brought us here."

Nate locked eyes with the boy and, grinning, slowly shook his head. "You're a bighearted fellow, Matthew m'boy, and God will bless you well for it."

The compliment seemed to draw the boy up taller, lift his chin, and throw out his chest with pride. "Guess what Emma's fixin' for Sunday dinner?" he asked, wiggling his brows mischievously.

Nate tapped a forefinger to his bearded chin. "Hmmm," he said, squinting as he sniffed the air, "can't say as I can place the aroma. Could it be a torn turkey that's bakin' in the oven?"

"You're close," said little Steven. "It's a bird, all right, but it doesn't say gobble-gobble. It says cluck-cluck!"

Giggling, Marcie clapped her hands. "Good one, Stevie! Good one!"

As though she were above all this childishness, Jenni rolled her eyes. "I made the stuffing," she announced. "And I baked a cake for dessert, too."

Nate raised both brows and patted his stomach. "Did you now? Well, young lady, if you have even one kind hone in your body, you'll quit talkin' about food, 'cause I skipped breakfast this mornin', y'know."

Emma, perched on the edge of a sofa cushion, gently bounced the baby on her knee. Casually, she leaned forward and, with her free hand, reached for the teapot. "Can I freshen your tea?" she asked Nate. "All these introductions haven't given you much time to drink. I'm sure it's cold by now."

He laid a hand atop hers, then eased her fingers from the handle. "My tea's just fine," Nate said, "and when 'tisn't, I'll pour m'self a second cup. You just sit back there and relax a mite, why don't you, and let us take care of you for a change?"

He began doling out instructions: "Jenni, m'darlin', has the table been set?"

The girl returned his grin. "Not yet."

"Well then, Marcie, you should get right on it. And Matthew, is there wood in the firebox?"

Matt took a deep breath, knowing in advance what his assignment would be. "C'mon, Ryan," he droned, "let's head on outside."

"Take Steven, there, with you," Nate called after them. "It's time he started learnin' how to stack a proper load in his arms."

When the children left the room, he sat beside Emma on the sofa and held one finger in the air. "Listen," he said, wide-eyed and grinning, "the silence is lovely, isn't it?" Once she nodded her agreement, he added in a whisper, "But not nearly so glorious as the sound of happy youngsters, though I would never admit it to one of 'em!"

Smiling, she inclined her head as if he spoken a foreign language. "You're a bighearted fellow, Nate m'man," she quoted in a perfect imitation of his Irish brogue, "and God'll bless you well for it."

Laughing softly, Nate filled her cup. He saw her drop a single sugar cube into her tea the last time they shared a meal. He added one to the brew now, and stirred it.

His heart stirred, too, as the vision in pink sat smiling beside him. She never married, never carried a child in her womb. But to Nate, Emma looked as natural holding a babe in her arms as a woman who had it in the usual way.

"So tell me how it 'twas that your little family grew twice in size since last I saw you," Nate said. And as she spoke, he leaned back and draped an arm across the seat back and listened to her explanation, marveling at the way she used her hands, her eyes, her smile to emphasize various aspects of the story.

What was it about this woman, Nate wondered, that made him behave like a completely different man in her presence? Here in her parlor, on his last visit, he cracked jokes like a stage performer, but alone in his room, he was more dour and dreary than a Tibetan monk. With Emma, he felt young and vital and alive; without her, he may as well have been a doddering old man.

"...And she's still a bit feverish, I'm afraid."

He'd been daydreaming, and hadn't heard a word of what she said. "I hope you'll forgive me bad manners, but I'm afraid me mind got to wanderin'. Would you mind tellin' your story again? I promise to pay attention this time."

The friendly smile never left her face as she wagged a scolding finger at him. "Am I so boring," she said with a flirtatious tilt of her head, "that I can't hold your attention for even a few minutes?" She held his gaze a moment before fussing with the baby's blanket. Satisfied it was tidy enough, she rested a hand upon the child's chest.

Nate rested a hand upon hers. "There are many words I'd use to describe you, Emma Wright," he said, "but boring certainly isn't one of 'em."

Her clear blue eyes blinked once, twice before he continued.

He started slow: "Beautiful; warm; friendly." And as his saw blade spun faster as more water powered the turbine, the praise pouring from his lips picked up speed: "Graceful; loving; talented; sweet; beautiful."

"You said 'beautiful' twice," she stopped him, giggling.

"It bears repeating, for you're not just easy on the eyes, you've got the heart and soul of an angel."

He watched as her cheeks flushed pink and her long lashes fluttered. His compliments embarrassed her, Nate realized *'Tis such a shame, for a woman like this should be accustomed to regular flattery!* Touched by her discomfort—and feeling slightly guilty for having caused it—Nate brushed her cheek with the backs of his fingers. "Finish your story, Emma," he said softly. "You have me word: I'll not let all the wonderful things you are distract me again."

She held his gaze, and he read the warmth in her eyes. *Oh, but I'd like to kiss you again, Miss Emma Wright, and feel your sweet arms wrapped 'round me.* He leaned forward, closer, closer, and Emma slowly closed her eyes.

And Becky began to squirm in her arms. "If I give her a bottle now," she said, standing, "perhaps she'll nap during dinner."

Nate shrugged. "'Tis no problem even if she doesn't. I've taken many a meal one-handed, workin' in me shop. I'd be happy to hold the little darlin' while you eat."

She headed for the kitchen. "I'll just heat up her bottle, then. Care to join us?"

As Nate followed on her heels, the girls rushed into the room. "The table is set, but the roasting pan is wedged in the oven," Jenni blurted.

"And the stuffing will burn if we don't take it out soon," Marcie added, jumping up and down.

Nate believed he could read Emma's thoughts as she looked from her temporary daughters to the stove to the baby: *I only have two hands,* she seemed to be thinking. *How am I going to heat up a bottle, tend the chicken, and hold the baby…all at the same time?*

"Hand over that baby," he said, bundling the infant to his chest. "I'll take her on a house tour while you get things under control in here. By the time we're back," he said from the hall, "you'll have her bottle warmed, and she'll have worked up a hearty appetite for it. And get that worried look off your face, darlin' Emma," he threw over his shoulder. "If anything goes awry, keep in mind that my sister had three babies in five years; I've likely powdered as many bums as you have!"

As he wandered the quiet, tidy rooms of Emma's home, Nate hummed softly into Becky's ear. It wouldn't be hard to imagine himself part of this happy household, where everything had a place, and everything was in its place.

In the boys' room, there were two beds, one a bit narrower than the other. No doubt Ryan and Steven shared the widest, while Matt slept alone. The bed covers and curtains were sewn of a green and rust cotton plaid. Underfoot, a shaggy knotted rug; on the night table between the beds, a polished brass lantern; behind the door, a series of wrought iron hooks where the boys could hang their shirts and trousers at night; against the far wall, a low-slung bureau that gleamed under a fresh coat of beeswax.

The girls' room—the largest upstairs—boasted a four-poster cherry wood bed that supported a double-wide feather mattress. Its coverlet was made of lacy white eyelet, and the curtains in the window matched it exactly. On either side of the bed, thick chenille scatter rugs warmed the floor, and a dainty pedestal table carved from the same gleaming wood as the bed held delicate crystalline lanterns. Behind their door, brass hooks held the girls' frilly skirts as they slept.

He was not the least bit surprised by the practical plainness of Emma's room, where a sleigh bed of golden oak dominated the space. A chiffarobe took up most of the short wall, a dressing table stood against the long one. At the windows were simple white cotton curtains, and on the bed, a bright patchwork quilt.

The day he'd made the minor repair in Stella's parlor, he took it upon himself to check the rest of the house for the squeaking hinges, loose doorknobs, and jammed windows that were so commonly left untended in a house without a man living in it. He found nothing, of course, for Emma had done a fine job keeping up with the smaller repairs before leaving on temporary assignment in Baltimore. She could easily leave this room for her aunt's larger one (she'd refinished and rearranged everything else since the funeral). Instead, she remained in the smallest room on the second floor, where the furnishings were simple and the ceiling dipped low. And Nate believed he knew why.

Each deep-set window seat overlooked a quiet street with an expansive view of the valley and the river and...

Wait...is that my shop over there? he wondered, leaning in for closer inspection. *Aye, that'd be the tin roof of the barn, all right.* He wondered for an instant if Emma knew that his home was visible from her window. "Not likely," he whispered to the baby. "She's not the type to sit and gawk out a window. Not with all she has to do in carin' for the lot of you young ones."

Half an hour later, when the commotion in the kitchen settled, Nate sauntered into the room. "I put her up over my shoulder," he said, handing her back to Emma, "and she gave a big healthy belch." Shrugging nonchalantly, he added, "She fell asleep suckin' her thumb. My sister would've pulled it away, sayin' that when her teeth came in they'd stick out like a beaver's." He stroked her downy-haired head. "But I left it there, 'cause I think this little one is entitled to a bit of pleasure in her life."

Emma peeked into the baby's diaper. "Nate," she said, eyes wide with astonishment, "you really do know how to change a baby!"

His heart did a flip in response to her delight. "'Twas nothin'. Just a matter of takin' off the wet one and replacin' it with a dry one." Grinning, he leaned forward to add "I realize you ladies have fairly well cornered the market on child care, but there are a few things we gents can do."

But her focus remained on the baby's pants. "Snug, but not too tight, and folded so neatly." Emma met his eyes to say, "Who taught you to—"

"If you watch a thing done a thousand times, it's bound to rub off on you."

"Rub off on you?" Matt interrupted. "Yuck!" he said, grimacing and holding his nose. "Why would you want any of that to rub off on you?"

Ryan's soft-spoken voice broke through the good-natured melee. "It's not so bad, Matt. 'Specially if you sorta turn your head and squint and hold your breath when you do it."

Matt's eyes widened and his lips drew back in shock. "You've changed dirty diapers?"

The boy nodded, then smiled up at Nate, as if proud to have even something so insignificant in common with the man.

"Whoa," Matt said, eyes closed and hands raised, "before I lose my appetite." To Emma he said, "Speaking of appetites, when's dinner?"

"I was just about to call all of you to the table when Mr. O'Neil came in with Becky. Have you washed your hands, children?" she asked, looking at each in turn.

Five heads dutifully nodded yes.

"Then...last one to the table is a rotten egg," Emma said, laughing as she darted into the dining room.

Amid shrieks and giggles of pleasure, Emma invited Nate to sit at the head of the table.

"Children," she said, clapping to get their attention, "settle down now. Mr. O'Neil is going to say the grace for us." She smiled sweetly. "You don't mind, do you?"

Nate honestly couldn't remember the last time he prayed over a meal. But he held her gaze and matched her smile. "Don't mind a bit."

He bowed his head and folded his hands, and when the children followed suit, Nate closed his eyes. "Dear Lord," he began, "we thank You for the food we're about to eat. Thank You for providin' it, and bless the dear woman and sweet girls who cooked it up. Keep us safe long after we've cleaned our plates. Keep us well, too, and near to You." He paused, then said, "Watch over our young friend, Curtis, and see that we have a chance to meet up with him from time to time. Amen."

When Nate looked up, he found Matt staring straight at him, a look of genuine gratitude on his young face. The expression turned mischievous as he said, "Will everybody please say 'Amen' so I can get somebody to pass the mashed potatoes? I'm famished!"

⌒

Nate insisted on helping with the dishes, despite her protestations. Afterward, to free Emma up to give Becky her bedtime bottle, Nate volunteered to tuck the rest of the children in.

If he knew part of the job included listening to their prayers, he might not have been so quick to offer, because each time one of their sweet voices asked God to bless him, Nate thought his heart might thump straight out of his chest. It touched him deeply, to be so completely accepted and included in their lives and hearts, for he hadn't done anything to earn such full-fledged devotion. But it was the same way with his sister's children: they, too, gave their trust and love openly and willingly. Treasured gifts, each and every one of them were treasured gifts. And in repayment, he believed, adults were charged by God Almighty to care for and protect those precious gifts.

When at last the older children were safe and snug in their beds, Nate descended the staircase, intent upon seeing how Emma was coming with Becky's feeding. He wasn't halfway down the stairs when Emma's sweet song, wafting up from the parlor, lulled him, lured him nearer. Standing out of sight near the parlor door, Nate listened with rapt attention.

> On angels' wings you'll ride, my love,
> > into the starry sky, where dreams are sweet and ever-
> > long, and God will kiss you, by and by.
> Your little head will rest, my love, on clouds of
> > snowy white, you'll sleep 'neath blankets,
> > soft and smooth, sewn of pale moonlight.
> You'll dream of rainbows, hearts, and flowers,
> > all through the midnight dark.
> And when the sunlight warms your face,
> > you'll wake to hear the lark.
> Then on angels' wings you'll ride, my love,
> > into my waiting arms, and through every
> > minute of the day,
> I'll keep you safe from harm.

When the song ended, his heart lurched with regret. *Sing another*, he wished silently. Nate waited a moment, then two, hoping the music of her voice would begin again. When it did not, he heaved such a great disappointed sigh that even Emma could hear it.

She looked up from the baby's sleeping face. "How long have you been standing there?" she whispered, smiling softly.

He gave no answer to her simple question. Instead, Nate walked quietly into the room and knelt at her feet. "Did I ever tell you that I once believed me own dear mother had the most beautiful female voice on God's green earth?" Gently, he laid a hand alongside her face.

She turned her face into it and, ever so lightly, kissed his palm. "Leave it to an Irishman," she said, grinning, "to answer a question with a question."

"Since first I laid eyes on you, I've asked myself what sets you apart from other women. Hearin' you sing gave me the answer: God has blessed you with ten times more grace and beauty than any—"

Emma laid a finger over his lips. "Shhh…you'll wake the baby."

For the first time since gripping the rocker's curved wooden arm, he looked at the sleeping infant. "Ah, but she's a darlin' little thing, isn't she?"

"Darlin'."

When he saw the mischief twinkling in her eyes, Nate stood, leaned down, and gripped both chair arms. "D'you know what it does to a fellow, seein' a woman with a babe in her arms?"

Her impish grin faded, and Emma shook her head.

"It makes him yearn to be that woman's man…and the child's da." He pressed a lingering kiss to her lips. "Now," he rasped softly, "put that young'un into her cradle…or I'll have no choice but to do it myself."

SEVEN

Nate, still on one knee, watched as Emma gently laid the sleeping baby into the cradle near the hearth, and fussed with the blankets. She was like no one he ever knew.

Laura, the young woman he'd almost married, was dark-haired, with deep-set dark eyes set in an almond complexion. Emma's golden hair shimmered like the sunbeams that skip across a wind-rippled pond, and her wide, long-lashed eyes, bluer than the summer sky, flashed when she talked, reminding him of the sparks produced by the bellows in his workshop.

Laura's straight nose pointed to narrow lips that routinely frowned as she considered methods of getting her way…and pouted when she didn't. Emma's nose, slightly broad, directed one's eyes to an enchanting full-lipped mouth that seemed to prefer a smile over every other expression. She'd broken her nose as a girl, as evidenced by the slight crook near her brow. Someday, Nate hoped to learn how it had happened.

Laura's delicate frame always made him fear a hearty hug could break every bone in her rib cage. But her petite body echoed her attitude, promising her man a lifetime of whimpering over one fragility or another. Emma, though tall and willowy, felt far, far sturdier in his arms than she looked!

While Laura's movements were quick and birdlike, Emma's were deliberate and graceful. Laura's hands had never plunged into a bucket of harsh detergent, never scrubbed grime from the knees of a boy's dungarees, never removed splinters or bandaged cuts… nor were they likely to. Emma's long-fingered, somewhat calloused hands were proof she never shied away from hard work. She was as comfortable swinging an ax as she was arranging daisies in a vase. Those hardworking fingers tenderly caressed Jenni's cheek, lovingly ruffled Matthew's hair, and, as she was doing now, making sure every wrinkle in Becky's bed was pressed flat by the warmth of her own two palms. Caring for others came as naturally to Emma as caring for herself came to Laura.

"Won't you come sit with me?" he invited, extending a hand. Grinning, Nate added, "That child is oblivious to your…" He quirked a brow. "What exactly are you doin' to her, anyway?"

Emma straightened, resting both hands on the edge of the cradle. "Why, I'm rubbing her, of course."

She said it as though rubbing a baby from head to toe was a most ordinary thing. Nate never saw his mother do it, nor Ian's wife, Mary, nor his sister Suisan. "Rubbin' her? Whatever for?"

She lit the floor lamp beside the sofa. "In case she has an itch," Emma said matter-of-factly, blowing out the match. "She's too small to scratch it herself."

She stood so near, Nate could smell the delicate scent of the lavender perfume she wore.

"If she were older," Emma continued, tossing the match into the fire, "Becky might ask one of us to relieve an itch she couldn't reach herself, but…"

Chuckling, Nate scrubbed his face with both hands. "You're priceless, Emma Wright," he said, grabbing her hand.

Emma studied his face, as if to determine whether or not he was poking fun at her.

"Leave it to you to think of such a thing. I don't imagine one mother in a thousand ever gave a thought to whether or not her infant might have an itch." He squeezed her hand gently. "But for you, the idea came like second nature."

She blushed. "Would you care for a cup of tea?"

"You can't change the subject that easy," he said, winking. "Besides, I've had enough tea this evening to float a boat." He patted the cushion beside him. "Now, for the love of good Saint Pete, won't you sit beside me?"

For the third time in as many minutes, Emma glanced at the cradle.

"She's safe and sound, all tucked in like a butterfly in a cocoon. Besides," he added, chuckling as he tugged her hand, "little Becky is but three feet away. If she so much as blinks, you're close enough to hear it!"

Emma started to make herself comfortable on the opposite end of the sofa, but Nate's hold on her forced Emma to sit near him. Without turning loose of her hand, he draped an arm across the sofa back.

Emma sank back against the cushions and, sighing, snuggled into his arm.

"This is my favorite time of day," she whispered.

"And why would that be?" he asked, massaging her shoulder.

"Because of the quiet," she said on a sigh. "It's as if the entire world is at rest."

Nate leaned forward slightly to better see her face. In the dim glow of the lantern light, her hair took on a burnished copper tone, her cheeks a rosy glow. Emma's long lashes dusted her high cheekbones as her voluptuous pink lips turned up slightly at the corners.

He pulled her closer, pressed a lingering kiss to her temple. "You're a vision, Emma Wright," he sighed. "Do you mind if I ask a very personal question?"

Her gentle smile became a teasing grin. "I'm afraid I can't answer that…until I hear the question."

Chuckling, he kissed her cheek. "How old are you?"

"I thought Irish mothers were the epitome of decorum. Didn't your mama teach you that that is the one question you should never ask a lady?"

"Ma joined the angels in heaven before the rest of us set foot on American soil. I'm afraid all she had time to teach me was that if I wanted answers to my questions, I'd better ask 'em, straight out."

"I learned the same lesson," she admitted, "from my moth… from my Aunt Stella. She taught me to appreciate folks who talk straight, because they don't come along often." Emma inhaled a shallow breath. "I'm twenty-eight…for a little while longer…which makes me Ellicott City's resident old maid." Giggling softly, she added, "Every town needs one of those, don't you know."

"What I know," he began, "is that the men in this town are either blind or stupid. Why hasn't one of 'em snapped you up?"

She shrugged. "Once, I believed I'd been born to become some fine man's wife and the mother of his children. But as the years passed, it became apparent no white knight would ride into town on a sturdy steed to carry me off to his castle. I came to the conclusion that since the dawn of time, men have needed to feel like the mighty protectors." She sat up a bit, wriggled her hand free of his grasp, and crossed both arms over her chest. "That's quite a feat when a woman matches—or exceeds—his height."

"Great Caesar's ghost," he interrupted. "There's no denyin' you're no wee slip of a thing, but you're not Jack's Giant, either."

Emma forced a deep voice and tucked in her chin. "'Fee, fi, fo, fum—I smell the blood of an Irishman….'" She punctuated her impression of the giant in *Jack and the Beanstalk* with a merry laugh. Her merriment faded when she added, "I suppose you're right. I'm not a giant, exactly, but..."

"But nothin'!" Nate drew her nearer still. "I'm five-feet-nine by the yardstick; you couldn't measure more than five-feet-seven, yourself." Shaking his head, he sighed in vexation. "I've come to a conclusion of my own: The unmarried men in this town *are* blind and stupid." *Because you're a woman, through and through*, he thought, *and if I weren't....If things were different, I'd marry you myself!*

"Flatterer," she said.

Nose to nose now, they gazed into each other's eyes for a long moment. "If those young ones weren't upstairs asleep," he growled, "I'd..."

One delicate eyebrow rose as she said "You'd what?"

"I'd kiss the daylights out of you, that's what," he said without thinking.

Now she raised both brows. "Oh, you would, would you?"

Nate studied her face, from the long-lashed gleaming eyes to the dimples in each cheek. Focused solely on her well-rounded lips, he grated, "Aye. I would."

"You are an amazing man, Nate O'Neil."

"Amazing?"

She nodded. "You make me feel so completely at ease that I believe I can tell you anything."

His breath caught in his throat as he watched her paint her lower lip with the tip of her tongue.

"Mmmm," he said distractedly. "Anyth—"

"Not another soul knows it, but my Aunt Stella was actually my mother."

That surprised him, but he tried not to show it. "Y'don't say?"

Emma nodded, and proceeded to tell him about the letter Horace Pickett had delivered those months earlier. Nate listened with rapt attention, understanding that she had shared a

well-guarded secret with him. It pleased him to know she trusted
him so.

"For a long while, the lie caused me a lot of pain. But the Lord
showed me that forgiveness is the most loving of human emotions.
I only wish Stella would have told me while she was alive, so she
could have died knowing it made no difference to me."

"She knows it now," Nate said. "Ma told me that when we die,
we arrive in heaven in the twinkling of an eye, and that once we're
there, our human frailties disappear, and we know everything that
was a secret before our death."

Smiling serenely, Emma nodded. "It's your turn," she invited.

"My turn?"

"To share a dark secret from your past."

Though her face beamed with mischief, Nate's heart thundered with fear and dread. How could he tell her, and risk having
her hate him?

"Alright," she said. "Another time, perhaps."

Relief coursed through him, and Nate relaxed, slightly.

"Now, where were we when I decided to confess my sin of
anger to you?"

Grinning, he moved in closer. "Somethin' about kissin' the
daylights out of you, if there weren't five youngsters."

Emma laid a finger over his lips to silence him. "They're very
sound sleepers."

Nate's brows rose slightly. *Surely she doesn't mean....*

Bracketing his face with both hands, she pressed her lips to
his.

And when she uttered a delightful, musical sigh, his heart
pounded like a parade drum. He slipped one hand beneath the
luxurious lengths of her silken hair and gently cupped the back
of her head. The fingertips of the other hand rested lightly on her
jaw, and his palm, resting on her long, slender neck, counted her
pulse beats.

Oh, to hold her this way for a lifetime, to hold the blissful sensation, borne on the wings of believing—even for this brief moment in time—that he was a decent man who deserved the simple comfort of a good woman's love. If only he could go back in time and undo all the evil he did!

Emma was everything he ever yearned for. His lonely heart ached to have her within arm's reach until he drew his last breath. Something told him that with Emma, anything was possible. If a full-scale shipbuilding business was his goal, he could reach it, with Emma at his side. If his dream was to out produce every wheelwright east of the Mississippi, it would have come true, if Emma was his wife.

She gave every task, regardless of how mundane and seemingly unimportant, her level best. A man would have to be addle brained not to know what a treasure he'd have in Emma Wright: A woman who put such time and thought into the placement of each doily and knickknack, who considered a helpless babe's unscratched itches, who served up a simple chicken dinner for her motherless charges as though President Lincoln himself sat at the head of the table, could give nothing but full-blown, all-out love to the man in her life.

Even this delicious kiss was proof that she did nothing halfway. Her sweet sigh told him that she grew to care deeply for him. Nate sensed that if he ended the kiss right now, and asked her to marry him, she'd say "Yes."

How can you even think such a thought, man! She deserves better than the likes of you, for if she grew to depend on you, as those men depended on you...

Images of that night flashed through his mind, from the blinding cannon blasts that lit the dark sky to the bloody bodies that darkened the soft green grass. With a guttural groan, he tore himself from the comfort of her embrace and stood abruptly. Driving both hands through his hair, Nate stared silently into the flames leaping in the hearth.

She was at his side in a heartbeat. "Nate...what is it?" Concern furrowed her brow as she laid a hand upon his forearm.

Shoulders drooping, he pocketed both hands. How could he tell her that he'd foolishly fallen in love with her? He suspected that she loved him, too, and he'd selfishly allowed it. How could he explain that, because of his past, their love was doomed, before it could begin? Heaving a great sigh, he said, "'Tis gettin' late, is all. I should be goin'."

Emma placed a hand on either side of his face and forced him to look directly at her. "Nonsense," she said, nodding toward the mantle clock. "It's barely eight." Then, inclining her head, Emma added, "It isn't healthy to keep things bottled up inside you." She smiled gently. "Now, why don't you tell me what's wrong?"

What's wrong, he wanted to say, *is that I'm a tainted man. If I had a shred of honor in me, I'd never have allowed this to get started.* Instead, he shook his head. "There's nothin' wrong, Emma. I'm... I'm thinking of your reputation, is all," he fibbed. "Those old crones in town will make a scandal of my visits, and you'll pay a price."

He watched as she studied his face. Her eyes flickered with fear and dread, confusion, embarrassment. "How thoughtless of me!" she said after a moment of intense scrutiny. "You put in a long, hard day before coming here. You're tired, aren't you?"

Aye, Nate thought, *I'm tired, all right. Tired of running from the shadow of death that's trailed me since that night.* He looked at her, and smiled sadly. *Ah, but Emma, I'm not tired of living. I'll never grow tired of a world with you in it.*

Nate saw no point in continuing this charade. He was no good for her. Period. *You can never be her husband, but you can be her friend.*

He tried to remember how many times he kissed her. Twice? Three times? He would treasure each one, always, for there would not be another. Thinking of the story he'd told Matt, about the mother who was willing to give up her baby in an attempt to do what was in his best interests, Nate traced the contours of her face. It wouldn't be easy, doing what was best for Emma. Nate knew that much already. But he would give up this ludicrous notion they could ever be more than friends.

"How'd you break your nose?"

Giggling, Emma hid her nose behind one hand. "Goodness," she said, "that certainly came from out of the blue!"

Nate repressed the heaviness growing in his heart. He would deal with his grief later, alone in his room. Right now, he'd see to her needs...as a true friend would.

He'd have to back off gently, though, because someday, the right man for Emma would come along. And if she kept thinking of herself as a gentle giant, she'd walk right past him. She told him that she'd dreamed of becoming a wife and mother, and he shared her belief that God intended her to marry and raise a houseful of children. If anyone deserved to see a dream come true, it was Emma!

Forcing a merry grin, Nate winked and tweaked her nose. "'Tis quite attractive. Gives you a look that tells the world you've lived life to its fullest."

Smiling, Emma tucked in one corner of her mouth. The happy light dancing in her eyes told him that his plan was working. His praises made her feel pretty and wanted, things she'd always deserved to feel. He would continue to dispense compliments to encourage this very feminine, very womanly reaction. Because in his opinion, it was only a matter of time before another man— one without a dishonorable past—noticed what a truly beautiful woman she was, and make Emma his bride.

Another man's lips pressed to hers. Another man's arms wrapped around her. The image stabbed through his brain like a hot poker, and it was all Nate could do to hide a grimace of pain. "So how'd you break it?" he asked again, changing the subject.

She perched on the sofa, and as he had moments earlier, Nate patted the cushion.

"I was out back in the apple tree," she said, sitting beside him, "and my foot slipped. I would have fallen straight to the ground if I hadn't hugged a branch." She laid a finger beside her nose. "Hugged it so tight, it broke my nose.

"I avoided mirrors for nearly a month," she added, rolling her eyes. "It wasn't bad enough I stood a full head taller than every boy in school, now I had ugly, swollen bruises all over my face, too. I looked like a raccoon!"

"The loveliest raccoon ever born, I'm sure," he said truthfully. Then, remembering his promise to back off gently, he said, "Broke my own nose when I was a scrawny lad," Nate said, chuckling. "But unlike you, I didn't avoid mirrors. Quite the contrary. I liked the rough-and-tumble look the bruises gave me."

"You? Scrawny? I don't believe it." She squeezed his bicep.

You're not goin' to make this easy for me, are you, Emma darlin'? he asked her silently. Emma seemed to know, instinctively, exactly what to say and do—and when—to make a man feel like the most powerful being on feet. He had to get out of here before....

She snuggled against his chest. "Nate..." she sighed. "Even your name is strong."

Lord God in heaven, he prayed, *give me the strength to leave here without—*

The prayer came a tick in time too late, for Emma had wound her arms around his neck and pressed another glorious kiss to his lips. *Remember, you promised to let her down easy,* he said to himself. *Ah, but mate, who'll let you down easy?*

In all honesty, he didn't want the kiss to end. Nate wanted to share his life with this loving woman. Wanted a home, wanted children with her, wanted to grow old and gray beside her. He could bear anything if she was beside him, even his memories of that night on the battlefield.

As he reveled in the nearness of her, Nate acknowledged a reality: Once, he'd craved the dizzying, lulling effects of alcohol. Emma affected him in much the same way, softening the rough edges, dulling the hurts, easing the stresses and strains of everyday life. It took a hundred dead men to make him give up the drink. Nothing short of the mighty power of God Almighty would make him give Emma up.

He admitted, in an odd and bitter moment, that he could not let her down easy, as he hoped. His weakness for whiskey was nothing in comparison to his need to be with this woman. Complete avoidance was the only way he knew to beat his monstrous craving for the elixir. And so....

When he left here tonight, he would not, *could* not return. Better for her to think herself too tall to be loved than to be sentenced to a lifetime, yoked to a haunted man.

EIGHT

He leaned casually on a post outside the bank, one pointy-toed boot crossed over the other, rolling a cigarette as he surveyed the comings and goings on Main Street.

Matt had seen him before, ambling around town, a wide-brimmed leather hat pulled low on his forehead, all but hiding black, shoulder-length hair that gleamed in the sunlight like a raven's wings.

He stood taller and broader than any man the boy had ever seen, including his own pa. Matt had no idea why the stranger came to town. He only knew that if he could emulate an adult, it'd be this one, who looked like one of the heroes in the novels he read.

The man stuck the cigarette into his mouth and struck a match on the heel of his boot. When the cigarette's tip glowed bright red, his dark eyes narrowed as a blue-gray haze of smoke curled around his face, reminding Matt of the snarling bank robber pictured on the wanted poster in the post office. The boy's heart raced when those black, hooded eyes zeroed in on him.

Matt quickly looked away, and pretended to be engrossed in a rowdy game of stickball taking place at the other end of the street. *One Mississippi, two Mississippi,* he counted, *don't look up 'til you get to ten Mississippi.*

Matt didn't know how the fellow managed to move in close without making so much as a whisper of a sound. But there he stood, thumbs hooked into his gun belt, a half smile slanting his thickly mustachioed mouth. He planted his big feet shoulder-width apart in the dusty street. And though Matt stood on the boardwalk, three steps up, he found himself inclining his head to meet the man's eyes.

"Something I can do for you, son?"

Even his voice was big and powerful! Matt repressed the urge to bolt and run. "N-n-no, sir."

Matt had read more than his share of dime Westerns. But none of the stories about cowboys and Indians and outlaws prepared him for this face-to-face confrontation with what could well have been a character straight from the pages of one of those novels.

With his thumb, the man shoved back his hat. "I've seen you around, several times. Do you live nearby?"

Matt's gaze darted left, toward Emma's house. As though hyp-notized, his arm lifted slowly and he pointed. "I...uh...I live right there."

Nodding, the stranger took note of the house. "Nice. Real nice. Reminds me of my granny's place." He unhooked one thumb from his gun belt and extended a meaty hand. "Name's Campbell. Hank Campbell. And yours?"

For an instant, Matt could only stare stupidly at the big, empty hand. After a moment, he realized what was expected of him, and held out his own. He'd always been big for his age, so it amazed Matt that his hand could all but disappear within Campbell's grip. "Uh...pleased to meet you, Mr. Campbell. My name is Matt. Matt Evans." He licked his lips. "Matt Evans Wright."

He had a quick, easy smile that put Matt's uneasy mind to rest. A little.

"The pleasure's all mine," the man said, winking. "But call me Hank. All my friends do."

Taking a last long drag from the cigarette, he flicked it onto the dusty street and ground it out with the sole of his boot. "How would you like to earn a nickel, Matt Evans Wright?" he asked, backing slowly away from the boardwalk.

Shrugging, Matt stepped down onto the next wooden step. "Doin' what?"

"Showing me around." Still moving gradually backwards, he glanced up and down the street before meeting Matt's eyes again. "Seems like a nice place. I might just like to stay awhile."

Matt stood in the street now. "A whole nickel," he said, falling into step beside Campbell, "just for showing you around this one-horse town?"

Campbell stopped, his smile dimming as he aimed a leather-gloved finger near Matt's nose. "This looks like a fine town, a good place to grow up. Don't ever be ashamed of your home, son, you hear me?"

Matt nodded. "Yes, sir, Mr. Campbell. I mean...Hank."

Campbell draped an arm across the boy's shoulders and led him down the road. "No time like the present, I always say." He shot Matt a sideways glance. "Unless you have chores to do for your mama."

Matt lifted his chin and squared his shoulders. "Don't have a mama," he announced. Nodding toward the tidy white house again, he added, "I've been staying with Miss Emma since I lost my family last September."

Campbell winced sympathetically. "Your ma and your pa and your little brother, all killed on the same afternoon." He shook his head. "Mmm-mmm-mmm. Now, that's a cryin' shame."

Matt shrugged. "It hasn't been so bad. Emma's a good substitute mother."

They walked a few steps in silence before Matt spoke again. "This is the feed and grain store," he said, pointing, "and over there is the post office."

If he'd been older and wiser, Matt might have read the man's calculating expression and known that nothing he said thus far was news to Hank Campbell. And he might have wondered how Hank had known that he'd lost his entire family on the same afternoon, too.

⁓

Farley stood on the steps outside his clinic, absently picking his teeth with a bit of straw as he watched Campbell and the boy march boldly down the street like long-lost friends. Shaking his head, he chuckled under his breath. *He may well be a nuisance*, the doctor told himself, *but he's worth every dime you're paying him. From the looks of things*, he added as the boy laughed heartily at something Campbell said, *he'll have the young'un eating out of his hand inside of five minutes. Won't need Nate O'Neil after all.*

He wondered what manner of deception Campbell would use to get the boy to go with him to Nebraska. Obviously, the man thought better of using Nate O'Neil in his plan to lure the children out of town. Campbell, it seemed, knowing the other children would do as Matthew said, had decided instead to buddy-up to the boy. Farley nodded his silent approval. *No sense getting more folks involved in the scheme than necessary.* He learned that, if nothing else, in his various business ventures.

He'd tried his hand at farming. But hard labor didn't suit him, so he rented the land to a man born to the work. He also tried running a hotel. But before that first week behind the counter ended, boredom convinced him to hire a live-in manager. Even operating his medical clinic hadn't satisfied him, and before long, Emma was doing all of the filing, ordering supplies, balancing the books, and a good deal of the doctoring, too.

Farley had to admit, it was quite a setup. He'd plunk down the cash to purchase a property, and after doling out a modest salary to each of his managers, the profits were his to spend or reinvest as he saw fit. *All the fun and none of the work*, he thought, smirking.

His most lucrative venture to date began on the train ride home from Richmond, when he met up with the Ohio farmer whose only topic of conversation was the children, riding in the passenger car ahead of theirs.

According to the rumpled, gap-toothed fellow, the parentless youngsters were heading north to Baltimore. There, they would change trains and travel west, where they'd be adopted by good Christian families in towns along the way.

"Couple of those boys looked strong enough to walk a day behind a plow without a meal or a night's rest," he'd said, sneering. Scratching his oil-slicked hair, he added, "I'd pay a pretty penny for one of 'em, I tell you, an' I know others back home who'd do the same. Cheaper than a hired hand, don't y'know."

At first, Farley bristled at the comment, especially coming from a man who claimed to be heading home from his father's funeral. But the more thought he gave the farmer's suggestion, the more attractive the idea became.

And at the whistle stop outside Baltimore, Farley promised farmer Ephram Hall that he would deliver one healthy boy for every five hundred dollars he could come up with. Seemed a perfect way to do a service for his country…and line his pockets with green at the same time.

The government was kicking in a healthy portion of the children's support. Didn't seem right that hardworking folks' tax dollars were being spent to care for other folks' young'uns, homeless or not.

He'd never liked children. They were, in Farley's opinion, needy, runny-nosed brats with dirty fingernails and whiny voices. They were messy and noisy and disrespectful. The only good use for them, as he saw it, was to work for their parents until they were old enough to pay their own way in life. And the farmer, in his own way, had all but admitted that he shared Farley's mind set.

"Here's my name and address," he'd said, handing Ephram Hall his card. "Those other farmers you spoke of...tell them I'll make them the same deal: I'll take five hundred a head for every healthy boy. Half that for girls." He'd snickered. "There are meals to cook and housework to do, don't y'know."

Hall had snickered, too. "That's a mighty steep price, don't you think?" Pocketing both hands, he stared Farley square in the eye. "I mean, once we sign for the young'uns, they're gonna cost us, for food and clothes and...."

"True enough," he agreed, "but when you buy a horse to pull the plow or a bull to put out to stud, you have to feed and house it, and the animal can only do one thing." He leaned in closer to add, "A son or a daughter can be trained to perform any chore that you find distasteful. And as you so astutely pointed out, they're cheaper than hired hands."

The farmer nodded, stroking his greasy beard as he considered Farley's words.

"You know I'm right," the doctor had grinned.

When Ephram Hall boarded the connecting train that would take him to Cincinnati, he winked and chuckled. "I'll think on it," he said, patting the pocket that held Farley's card. "Maybe you'll hear from me, and maybe you won't."

As Farley watched the train chug out of sight, he made a bet with himself: *Two months from now, old Ephram Hall will likely have himself a brand-spanking new son and a daughter.*

In half that time, a telegram arrived from Ohio, and to the unpracticed eye, it appeared to be an ordinary livestock order. Nothing suspicious about that, since Farley's tenant farmer was doing a fine job raising prized bulls on that stretch of land north of Baltimore.

Ship product as discussed. Stop. Two males, two females. Stop. Partial payment deposited to the bank of your choice. Stop. Final payment on delivery. Stop. Please wire ahead to schedule pickup. Stop.

And the sender was none other than Ephram Hall.

In the interim, Farley took the liberty of contacting the Children's Aid Society in New York. And the good ladies who ran the charity shot off a chatty letter, telling Farley how thrilled they were to have Ellicott City's only doctor and deacon of the King's Way Church assisting them in finding homes for children, orphaned by the war.

The first transaction with the Ohio farmers proved how easy it could he. *Rather like taking candy from babies*, he'd thought at the time. Within two months, he'd helped place a dozen children on farms and ranches out West. Some, Farley was certain, ended up in good homes with loving families. Others, it could only be presumed, wound up with parents like Ephram Hall, whose intention was never been to adopt a child, but rather to buy a slave. Either way, it was none of Farley's concern. He was far too busy putting a balance to the law of supply and demand…and increasing his bank account.

And until recently, when the half dozen brats who'd boarded the train in Richmond—and disappeared somewhere between there and Baltimore—his little money making scheme had been running quite smoothly. The only explanation, in his mind, was that the unhappy youngsters already placed were somehow warning the children still in orphanages back East.

Sooner or later, every child orphaned by the war would find homes. Farley knew he had to act fast, before the supply ran out. And if he hoped to sidestep this latest glitch in the works and accomplish his goal, he needed help.

Most recently, a Nebraska rancher had offered a thousand dollars for boys and five hundred for girls…and he'd ordered two of each! Even after paying Campbell off, the doctor would be able to make a sizable deposit in his bank account, thanks to the business he lovingly referred to as Child Find.

He'd read that developers were building comfortable cottages on the beaches in sunny Florida. Once this last transaction was concluded, Farley would withdraw his considerable savings and reserve a whole sleeper car on the next train heading south.

And Hank Campbell was his ticket out of town.

He was loading his wagon outside the feed and grain when he spied the doctor alone on the steps of his clinic, gaze fused to Campbell and Matthew. *What's his interest in those two?* Nate wondered as Farley's shifty eyes followed every move the man and the boy made. There was no logical explanation for the suspicion and mistrust swirling in the pit of his stomach. It wasn't until Farley closed the clinic door behind himself that Nate asked himself what Campbell and Matthew were doing together. He had no reason to mistrust Campbell, either, and yet...

It was an effort to appear nonchalant as he sauntered across the street and caught up with them. "Matthew," he said, falling into step on the other side of the boy. "Where are you off to on this fine spring day?"

The three stopped walking as Matt smiled innocently. "I'm showing Mr. Cam...I mean Hank...around town." Glancing at the taller man, he added, "He thinks he might like to stay awhile."

When Nate's gaze connected with Campbell's, a chill shot up his spine. He recognized the expression glittering in his dark, brooding eyes, for he'd seen it in the mirror, every time he trimmed his beard: Guilt? But what did young Matthew have to do with it?

Something was wrong here, very wrong, and Nate aimed to get to the bottom of it. To Campbell, he said, "So tell me, d'you think you'll be buyin' a farm outside of town? Or is ownin' a business down on Main Street more to your likin'?"

The man's heated gaze fused to Nate's. "I'm just in the 'considering' stage at this point," he said dryly. Campbell smirked over Matthew's head. "Why? You lookin' to sell your shop?"

Nate feigned a good-natured chuckle. "Not on your life," he said, grinning. "It's not only my livelihood; it's where I live, as you well know."

Campbell nodded. "I'm sure the long hours and the hard work help dim the memory of your past."

The only visible reaction to Campbell's stinging remark was the muscle that constricted in Nate's jaw. Hopefully, the beard hid it. But he refused to give this man the satisfaction of knowing he'd hit the intended target. "Idle hands are the Devil's workshop, my sainted ma used to say."

"Still…I don't suppose there's much you can do about the nights." Smirking, he raised one brow. "Does that battle haunt your dreams, O'Neil?"

The comment cut him to the quick, forcing him to look away. He sensed that if Campbell saw the pain in his eyes, he was doomed. Had the man come to town for no purpose other than to torment him? Perhaps he had a score to settle because he lost a brother or a lifelong friend on that battlefield. If that was the case, Nate believed he had no choice but to endure Campbell's wrath.

But something told him Campbell's presence had little, if anything, to do with that night in Chattanooga. His instincts told him talking of the battle was nothing but a means to an end. What end, Nate didn't know. It would take time and patience, but he'd get to the bottom of this if it was the last thing he did.

Time, he had an abundance of, now that he decided to stay away from Emma. Patience was another thing entirely. Nate had never been a particularly patient man, but prayer, he believed, would help him gather what he needed of it. Meanwhile, he would have to exercise care and caution.

"Still fighting your battle with the bottle?"

From the corner of his eye, Nate saw Matthew's brow furrow with confusion. He cut off a thumb rather than see disappointment on the boy's face. If Matt hadn't been standing between them, he might just box Campbell's ears. But he felt a certain responsibility to set a good example for Matthew, and how could he do that if he behaved like a hot-tempered oaf? "Haven't had a drop in more than a year."

He knew in the next heartbeat that Campbell had heard— and made note of—his slight hesitation. The man could never earn a living gambling. Not with a face that was so easy to read.

"I'll bet you miss the whiskey, don't you?"

That was truer than Nate cared to admit, but he dared not. "Nah." He would have pointed out that Campbell, too, had shown a real fondness for whiskey. But Nate didn't want Matthew hearing any more about his past. "Tell me, Matthew," he said, changing the subject, "how's little Becky doing?"

The boy regarded him through narrowed eyes. "Her fever broke, and Emma says she's going to be just fine." He paused before saying, "I didn't know you were in the war."

Nate would have said it was a subject he preferred to avoid. But Campbell beat him to it.

"Right up to the end! He and I were the only survivors of the bloody battle in Chattanooga. O'Neil, here, spent months in the infirmary recuperating from his wounds, and when they let him put his uniform back on, he became a courier."

Matthew's eyebrows rose. "What's a courier do?"

"Why, it's just about the most dangerous job a soldier can have." For an instant, genuine admiration beamed in his eyes. But quick as it appeared, Campbell blinked it away. "Sometimes, a courier is forced to run straight through the thick of things to deliver messages."

"Messages?" the boy asked. "What kind of messages?"

"Battle plans, warnings," Campbell explained. "Without the couriers, the leaders couldn't defend against attack."

Matthew's gaze locked on Nate's face. "You risked your life so the generals would know where the enemy was?"

Nate's ears and cheeks grew hot with shame. Bravery wasn't the reason he'd volunteered for the job—quite the contrary. After what he'd done, he believed he didn't deserve to live. Since he couldn't bring himself to put a gun to his own head, he became a courier in the hopes the enemy would do it for him.

The boy grabbed his arm. "Then you're a hero, Nate. A hero!"

Campbell's posture reflected his attitude. He stood, booted feet shoulder-width apart, hat shoved high on his head and his thumbs tucked into his gun belt. Nate didn't have to look up to read what was written on the man's face. *Hero, my six-toed foot!* Campbell was no doubt thinking.

"I'm no hero, Matthew, of that you can be sure. 'Twas the men who died. *They're* the heroes."

Suddenly, as though waking from a trance, Matt said, "Oh, my goodness! What time is it?"

Campbell nodded toward the big clock tower in the middle of the street. "If that's right, it's going on noon." Winking, he gave Matthew a playful shove. "What's the matter, son, you goin' sparkin'?"

The boy rolled his eyes and wrinkled his nose. "Not on your life! I wouldn't be caught dead alone with a girl. But Emma asked me to bring a few things home for supper, and I was supposed to pick up my pay at Mrs. Henderson's first, use it to buy flour and sugar and…"

Reaching into the pocket of his fringed suede jacket, Campbell withdrew a shiny silver dollar and tucked it into Matthew's hand.

The boy gasped as his mouth dropped open. He stared at the gleaming coin, balanced on his palm. "But…but you said…you said a nickel."

With a sideways nod, Campbell said, "Consider it an advance." Playfully, he mussed Matt's hair. "Next time we meet, you'll finish the job you started today." He held out his hand. "Deal?"

The boy shook the man's hand. "Deal!" To Nate, he said, "Emma told me if I saw you, I should tell you to stop by. You forgot something after dinner yesterday."

At the mere mention of her name, Nate's heart throbbed. He swallowed and frowned, hoping he'd caught himself in time to keep Campbell from seeing that he was sweet on Emma Wright.

"Forgot something? But what?"

Matt shrugged. "She didn't say. But she told me to tell you she put it in a safe place."

He wouldn't be stopping by her house to retrieve the forgotten item, no matter what it might be. He couldn't. They lived less than a mile apart, and he expected that from time to time, he would run into Emma in town. He'd be cordial when it happened, and nothing more, because he fully intended to stick to his promise to protect her from his past.

"Why don't you bring it by my shop," he suggested. "There'll be a bit of a treat in it if you do."

Matt pocketed Campbell's coin, as if to say there wasn't much that could compete with a whole silver dollar. "Sure, Nate," he said, walking backwards. "See you later!" With a smile and a wave, he turned and broke into a run.

Nate and Campbell stood side by side, watching as Matt drew closer to the store. Without looking away from the boy, Campbell said, "O'Neil, you old dog you, why didn't you tell me you had a sweetheart in town?"

Fighting a scowl, Nate bit out, "Because I don't."

Campbell's head swiveled until his gaze locked with Nate's. Jerking a thumb in the direction of Emma's place, he said, "But the boy said you had Sunday dinner with her. That you left something behind." He smirked. "Sounds to me like you planted it, so you'd have an excuse to go back and fetch it."

Campbell stared in the direction of her house. "Not that I blame you." Wiggling his brows and smacking his lips, he added, "Mmm-mmmmmm, she's one fine-looking lady."

Nate's hands balled into hard fists at the suggestive tone of Campbell's voice. *I oughta beat you senseless for even thinkin' such a thought.* "She's a good woman with a heart o' gold," he grated, "and there's not a man in this town who deserves the likes of her."

With the thumb and forefinger of his right hand, Campbell stroked his thick mustache. As if Nate hadn't spoken at all. "You say she's not your girl?"

Through clenched teeth, he said, "She's not me girl."

Campbell nodded in the direction Matt had gone. "Wish me luck, then," he said, two fingertips touching the brim of his hat in a jaunty salute, "not that I'll need it."

NINE

Emma was never formally introduced to Ellicott City's newest resident, but she could hardly have missed spotting him. Alongside the town's shopkeepers and farmers, he stood out like a preacher in a saloon.

Their collarless shirts, mostly white, were sewn of sturdy cotton, while Hank Campbell wore a pullover made of fringed deer hide. The townsmen held up plain black trousers with suspenders, whereas Campbell kept his buckskin pants up with a length of hemp. Ellicott City's finest wore ankle-high, thick-soled shoes that laced up the front, and Campbell slid his feet into pointy-toed snakeskin boots with tall, tapering heels made to slide easily into a saddle's stirrup. If they wore hats at all, the men in town chose narrow-brimmed derbies and fedoras. And a hat that could shade two heads perched low on Hank Campbell's head.

And oh, what a head it was, she admitted.

Gleaming hair, as black as ink, spilled down his back and over his shoulders, and a dark bushy mustache shaded his ample lower lip. Lushly lashed eyes that glittered like coal stared hard from beneath well-arched sable brows. A patrician nose bespoke his British heritage, while high cheekbones proved his Shawnee roots.

Emma had never seen a taller, broader man. Why, even she had to look up the day she came face-to-face with the handsome stranger. *Was it only a week ago?* she wondered, watching now as his thick legs carried him closer to her gate, a large brown package under each muscular arm.

She was in the post office, mailing a package to her cousins in Pennsylvania when a huge, looming shadow darkened the space around her. He did nothing more than stand in the doorway, she quickly realized, yet the size of him was enough to block the light coming through the entrance.

He smiled flirtatiously, touched two fingers to the underside of his hat brim, and said in a voice a full octave deeper than any she heard before, "Good morning, ma'am. Lovely day, isn't it?"

Emma didn't know if it was his size or the sound of the manly voice that intimidated her. She only knew that something about him frightened her. "Yes, lovely," she'd agreed.

Then he'd sauntered up beside her and leaned an elbow on the counter. "Springtime has always been my favorite season—spent a fair number of years in the Southwest. They're lucky to get anything but summer weather there."

Despite his friendly manner and conversational tone, her angst grew. What was it about him, she wondered then, as now, that set her pulse to pounding and her heart to racing with trepidation? The eyes, she decided, those dark, brooding eyes put the fear in her, for the smile that widened his mouth never warmed his cold, calculating orbs.

Now, as he moved closer to her front door, Emma hugged herself to ward off the chill his presence sent up her spine. "What on earth could the man possibly want?" she asked herself, squinting through the gauzy parlor curtains.

"Looks like you're going to find out soon enough," came Jenni's reply. "He'll be ringing the bell any second now."

The words were no sooner out of the girl's mouth than the doorbell jangled, cracking the quiet morning. Emma lurched with fright.

"Goodness gracious sakes alive," Jenni said, giggling softly. "You'd think he was a bandit or something, the way you're behaving. Matthew says Mr. Campbell is a very nice fellow."

"Nice. Yes," she responded distractedly. Smoothing her apron and tucking a loose tendril of hair back into her bun, Emma walked purposefully toward the front door. She stood in the foyer for a moment, closed her eyes, and took a cleansing breath. "Lord God Almighty," she prayed under her breath, "let him leave as quickly as he came."

She jerked open the door and forced a bright smile. "Mr. Campbell," Emma said in the friendliest voice she could muster, "what brings you here?"

With a nod, he indicated the sacks under each arm. "Overstocked my pantry, and being a man who hates to see anything good go to waste," he said with a suggestive quirk of his brow, "I thought perchance you could use these."

Emma glanced at the parcels. "I don't know what you may have heard, Mr. Campbell, but I have no need for your charity."

On another man, the boyish pout would have looked ridiculous. But on his handsome face, the hangdog expression was almost charming—almost.

"It isn't charity, Miss Wright. You'll be doing me a favor, taking the groceries off my hands." He tilted his head slightly. "And all I heard," he added, "was that Emma Wright treats everybody like family."

Sacks of flour and cornmeal and sugar poked out of the overstuffed bags. The truth of the matter was that she needed these things desperately. Swallowing her pride, Emma did what was best for her children: "Forgive me, Mr. Campbell," she said, waving him inside. "It's not every day a gentleman shows up at my door, arms overflowing with food."

"Which way to the kitchen? This load's getting a tad heavy."

She led the way down the hall. Gratitude made her feel obliged to say, "I just brewed a pot of tea. Would you care for a cup?"

"Don't mind if I do," he said, turning a chair around and straddling its seat as he faced the table. Campbell glanced around the sunny room. "Nice place you've got here. Makes a body feel welcomed, just setting foot inside."

She just placed a spoon beside his cup. "Why, thank you. What a nice thing to say."

He shrugged. "It's the plain truth, that's all."

Emma filled his cup, then hers. "One lump or two?" she asked, holding the sugar bowl in one hand and tiny silver tongs in the other.

"Two, if you don't mind."

She dropped the sugar cubes into the steaming liquid. "So how do you like our little town so far, Mr. Campbell?"

"I like it fine, Miss Wright." His big warm hand encircled her wrist. "But I'd like it even better if you called me Hank."

His grip was surprisingly gentle, but startled her nonetheless. After a moment of intense scrutiny, he released her. Emma sat stiff-backed across from him. "What brings you to Maryland, Mr. Cam...Hank?"

Another shrug. "Just passing through." He leaned closer. "Sometimes, in my travels, a place just fits, if you know what I mean."

"Can't say as I do," she admitted. "I was raised right here in this house. The farthest I've traveled is Baltimore. Well, except for a short trip to Lancaster as a girl."

"You're barely more than a girl now," he injected, winking. "When did you take this trip? Last week?"

His flattery seemed crude and insincere in comparison to Nate's compliments. She had no reason to dislike this man, but she disliked him nonetheless, and wanted the visit to end. Now.

"I think I hear the baby crying."

Campbell narrowed one eye, as if straining to hear what she heard. "Must've been a cat," he said, aiming that cold hard stare at her. "And speaking of babies, how many young'uns do you have?"

Emma flushed. "None of my own, as I'm sure you've heard. There are six children in my charge right now." Smiling sadly, she added, "There would be seven, but I found a home for one."

Nodding, his face gentled. "Life would be easier, I reckon, without all these children underfoot. I don't suppose you had a problem seeing to your own needs on your nurse's salary."

"I'm surprised to hear how much you know about me. It's a bit unnerving, I don't mind admitting, particularly since I know nothing about you."

He extended his arms "Hank Campbell, free spirit," he said, wearing a grin that was more a snarl. "Ex-soldier, ex-cowpoke, ex-Texas ranger. No wife, no young'uns, no living relatives. What more would you like to know?"

When you'll be leaving, for starters, she thought. But in place of an answer, Emma sipped her tea. Returning the cup to its saucer, she said, "You're right. Money was never tight when I had no one but myself to look after. But despite having to stretch a penny farther, I've never been happier."

"I was told you were a good woman, with a heart of gold. He was dead-on about you, Miss Emma Wright."

He? She blinked. She swallowed hard. Nate said those very words to her, just yesterday. "You were told...by whom?"

"Ran into an old army buddy in town. Nate O'Neil?"

Emma brightened at the opportunity to learn more about the man she loved. "You served during the war with Nate?"

"Spent nearly six months fighting alongside him. Nearly died alongside him a couple of times, too."

Furrowing her brow, Emma sighed. "It was a horrible, bloody war that should never have been fought. So many people suffered. So many are still suffering."

"The children, you mean?"

Nodding, she wrapped her palms around her cup. "Some of them stood by, helpless, and were forced to watch as their fathers and brothers were murdered. Others came home from school to find the slaughtered remains of their families." She took a deep breath, then let it go. "It seems so unfair."

Matt breezed into the room, oblivious to the topic of conversation. "Say, Mr. Cam…I mean Hank. What're you doin' here?"

"Well, son," he began, laughing good-naturedly as he leaned both elbows on the table. "Like the village idiot, I went and bought too many supplies. The flour and cornmeal will be overrun with weevils and the sugar will get hard as a rock by the time I get around to using all of it up. Your lovely substitute mother, here," he nodded in Emma's direction, "agreed to take it off my hands."

Matt's blue eyes brightened. "Now you can bake cookies for my lunch bucket! And corn bread for supper. And—"

"Whoa, there, Matthew," Campbell interrupted, one hand in the air. "She isn't your personal cook, you know. She has her hands full, taking care of the lot of you. It's costing her a fortune to feed and clothe you all. Can't you see how tired she is, worrying about how to make ends meet, trying to get everything done so you'll be well cared for? Why, just look at those dark circles under her eyes."

As if seeing her for the first time, Matt looked at Emma. "Maybe you could make the corn bread," Campbell suggested, "and Jenni can bake the cookies, so Emma will have a moment to put her feet up and relax for a change."

In place of Matt's happy smile, a worried frown appeared. "I'm sorry, Emma. Honest. I never meant to be so much work and expense."

Emma leapt from her chair and wrapped him in a motherly hug. "Matthew Evans Wright, I won't listen to another word of this nonsense," she scolded lovingly. Over his head, she glared at Campbell. "Mr. Campbell means well, I'm sure, and I appreciate that, but he's new here. He has no way of knowing how much joy you've brought to my life…how much pleasure all the children have given me."

Holding him at arm's length, she gave Matt a gentle shake. "I couldn't love you more if you were my flesh and blood son. There's nothing I wouldn't do for you, Matt, nothing! Do you hear?"

She watched as the boy nodded and forced a smile, and she loved him all the more for his brave pretense. Campbell's words stirred up something dark and dangerous in Matthew's still-healing heart, and Emma had a feeling it would take days to undo the damage the stranger had done.

"Where's Jenni?" Matt wanted to know.

"Helping Mary O'Neil around the house. Her baby is due any day, you know."

Again he nodded. "And Ryan and Steven?"

"In the schoolyard, I imagine." She smoothed the cowlick at the crown of his head. "You know how those two love to play stickball."

"What about Marcie?"

Emma laid a hand alongside his cheek. "She's out back, trying to teach that scruffy kitten she found in the alley last week to sit up and beg." She turned Matt around and gave him a gentle shove. "Now, why don't you run upstairs and check on little Becky for me while I see Mr. Campbell to the door?"

Without a word, the slump-shouldered boy did as he was told. As soon as he was out of earshot, she placed both hands on her hips and faced Hank Campbell, who'd stood when he heard her say she'd soon be showing him out. His size and might meant nothing to her now. The only thing that mattered was that his thoughtlessness had alarmed her boy.

"What I said to Matt bears repeating, Mr. Campbell: while I appreciate your concern, I'll thank you to leave the discipline of my children to me."

He opened his mouth to defend himself, but Emma's raised hand silenced him.

"If your meddling in matters that are of no concern to you is the price for those groceries, then you can just pack them up and find someone else to 'help' dispose of them, because I'll not have you undoing all the healing poor Matthew has done!"

The bewildered expression on his face told her that Hank Campbell was not accustomed to being scolded or left speechless, and Emma accomplished both with a few well-chosen words.

"Forgive me, dear lady," he said quietly. "I didn't mean any harm." He gave a slight shrug and held his hands out, palms up, in a gesture of helplessness. "Guess I have a lot to learn about young'uns, eh?"

An apology was the last thing she would have expected from this gruff, tough man. His words—and the sheepish grin on his face—cooled her ire. A little. Still, something about him troubled her. Emma wanted him out of her house as quickly as possible. But how would she accomplish it without appearing rude and ungrateful?

As if on cue, Becky cut loose with a loud, healthy wail. "Much as I've enjoyed our little chat," she said as she led him to the door, "I'm afraid someone needs her diapers changed."

Chuckling, he shook his head. "Fascinating as it sounds, I believe I'll take my leave." Standing in the foyer, he pulled open the front door. "Thanks for the tea," he said from the porch. "I hope I haven't worn out my welcome, because I enjoyed our chat, too."

"I'm sure we'll be seeing a lot of each other, especially if you decide to settle down in Ellicott City," she said, one hand on the knob. "Thank you so much for the food. It'll help out a lot, I can assure you. I'll send some corn muffins with Matthew."

When the closed door separated them, Campbell felt a notice-able chill. He knew better than to make a derogatory remark about a woman's appearance, regardless of how insignificant. But the purpose of his visit had not been to start a courtship growing, but to start Matthew's guilt growing, so he could make good use of it later.

And, to raise O'Neil's hackles, he'd insinuated that he thought Emma was one fine woman. He should have exercised some patience, and saved the comment for after he sat down for a face-to-face with her.

Because while he hadn't meant a bit of it earlier, he meant every word now.

His sister-in-law stood beside him at the table and laid a hand on his shoulder. "Why don't you talk to us about it, Nate?"

"There's nothin' to talk about, Mary."

"Nonsense," Ian said. "You've been down in the mouth for nearly a week now. Reminds me of the way you behaved when you first came to town. Now, out with it, Nathan—or do I have to take a strap to you?"

Ordinarily, the taunt was guaranteed to inspire a grin. But these were not ordinary times.

"It pains me to see you so sad, Nathan." Mary sat across from him at the kitchen table. "And you know what they say about expectant mothers."

Nate warmed in the glow of her loving smile. "Who's 'they'?"

"Why, the doctors, who else?"

Chuckling despite his foul mood, he took her bait. "All right, what do the doctors say about expectant mothers?"

Resting her chin on a doubled-up fist, Mary grinned. "That we're to stay calm and happy this close to the end, to prevent a catastrophe durin' the birth. You're worryin' me, Nate," she added, shaking a finger in his direction. "If the pain gets too bad, I'm goin' to hold you personally responsible!"

"Leave it to you to put things in their proper perspective," he told her. And to his brother, he said, "I'll not bear the burden of your handiwork, Ian. If anyone's responsible for the pain she's gonna feel, it's you!"

The three laughed...until Mary clutched her stomach and grimaced. "Praise the heavens," she said, half-standing, "I do believe it's time."

Nate and Ian stood, too, and hovered protectively on either side of the diminutive woman.

"Time?" Ian echoed.

"For your baby to be born, darlin' husband." She squeezed his hand affectionately. "Now be a good man, why don't you, and go and fetch the doctor."

Ian gripped Nate's shoulders and shook him hard. "You fetch Farley. I'm stayin' with me wife."

Mary straightened fully and exhaled a relieved sigh. "Well thank the Good Lord that's over...for the time bein', at least." She waddled up to her husband and took both his hands in her own. "Ian, m'darlin', I know your heart's in the right place, but you're white as a ghost. The walk into town will—"

"You'll be needin' as much air as you can spare in the next few hours, so save your breath. I'm not leavin', do y'hear?"

She sighed heavily and faced Nate.

"Much as I'd like to help you, Mary, there's no use talkin' to him when he gets this way." Nate hurried toward the door. "Put him to work boilin' water or makin' bandages of headsheets or somethin', so he won't drive you mad whilst I'm gone."

"Boilin' water and makin' bandages!" she repeated, giggling. "What do you think I'm about to do here, Nathan O'Neil, come apart at the seams?"

Nate had been nearby when Ian drew his first breath, and when each of his sister Suisan's babies fought their way into the world, too. He'd hadn't been mature enough to understand the miracle of birth back then, but this time, he realized the seriousness of this miraculous life process. If anything happened to Mary....

Blanching, Nate backed through the doorway. "Ian, don't just stand there with your tongue draggin' the floor," he said, grabbing the doorknob, "get your wife to bed. I'll be back with the Doc just as quick as I can."

He ran the entire mile and a half from Ian's house to the clinic. Farley's fancy black buggy was nowhere in sight. *Isn't it just like him to be off traipsing around when Mary needs him*, Nate thought, thundering up the wooden steps.

He didn't knock or ring the bell, or call out in a polite voice to announce his arrival. Nate barged through the door like a rampaging bull, and stood gasping in the entrance. If the long run hadn't taken his breath away, the vision before him would have.

Emma sat at Farley's desk, rocking Becky's cradle with one hand as she added numbers in her ledger book with the other. She tied back her long, silken hair with a black satin ribbon that matched the trim of her pale yellow dress, and looked like a ray of warm, refreshing sunshine.

She directed her first comment to the baby. "Well, will you look at what the wind blew in." And, calm as you please, she grinned mischievously. "I was beginning to think perhaps those people in Columbus's day were right," she told him, "and the world is flat after all, because it seemed you'd fallen off the face of the earth."

He'd stayed away with good reason, and felt guilty and miserable about it. But this was no time to be thinking of himself. "It's Mary," he said, breathing easier now. "Her baby's comin', and she needs the doctor."

Emma stood and, beaming, clasped her hands under her chin. "Oh, how wonderful for her and Ian. Their firstborn is about to arrive!" Quickly, she gathered her professional composure. "But Dr. Farley isn't here. I'm afraid you'll have to make do with me."

"There isn't a doubt in my mind that you can handle it every bit as well as Farley." He nodded toward the cradle. "But what about little Becky, there? And the rest of the young'uns?"

Emma breezed past him. "There isn't a doubt in my mind that you can handle them every bit as well as I can. I'll leave you to gather the rest of the children and bring them to Mary and Ian's house." She grabbed her medical bag, then scooped the baby up in her arms. "I'll bring Becky with me and hand her to Ian. Caring for her will keep his mind of Mary's labor. Besides," she said, grinning, "he needs the practice."

Until he burst through that door just now and caught his first glimpse of her in a week, he hadn't realized how much he'd missed her. *You've got to be strong, man*, he cautioned himself, *or you'll never stay true to your promise.*

"You're lucky this isn't a race, Irish, because I've gotten a head start."

Chuckling under his breath, he wondered when she'd taken to calling him "Irish." He caught up to her. *Ah, but she could charm the leaves from the trees*, he thought, smiling as she chattered all the way to Ian and Mary's house.

"It's lunchtime, so you'll need to feed the children, first."

Feed them? "I'm not much of a cook."

She waved his admission away. "They're not fussy. They'll eat rocks if you seasoned them."

And then she was gone.

He walked to her place and found the children, playing in the back yard. How excited they were to hear Mary's baby was about to be born! It was all they talked about as they gobbled up the buttered bread he served them for lunch. All they talked about as they walked to his brother's house, too.

They hadn't been inside ten minutes when Emma stepped out of the bedroom, took one look at Nate, and grabbed his hand. "Wipe that worried expression from your face, Irish, unless *want* to scare your brother and Mary!"

"I had no idea I was looking—"

She gave his cheek an affectionate pat. "You look like you've come face-to-face with the Angel of Death. Mary is having a baby, the most natural and normal thing a woman can do. She's healthy and strong, so there's absolutely no reason to be afraid. Now, smile! You're about to become an uncle for the fourth time. You have every reason to be happy, too!"

If he was thinking rationally, he would never have given in to the temptation to hug her.

"Yrr crhhhg me," Emma mumbled.

"What's that?"

"Yrr crhhhg me," she repeated. And pressing her free hand against his chest, she gave a mighty shove. "I said 'You're crushing me!'"

He held her at arm's length. "Sorry. Guess I have a lot to learn about—"

"What're the two of you babblin' about over there?" Ian shouted from the porch. "Mary's havin' another pain, and this one is nothin' like the first."

Now Emma's face registered concern. As she raced inside, Emma called over her shoulder, "You might want to let your father know what's going on. I'm sure he would like to be near when his newest grandchild is born."

For a reason Nate couldn't explain, a sense of peace enveloped him, just knowing Emma was in charge. It took a moment for it all to sink in, and when it did, Nate swallowed hard. He gathered up all the children and bundled Becky into his arms, and headed for his father's cottage on the outskirts of town. Half an hour later, with his father and Emma's orphans trailing behind him in a single file, he grinned despite himself. "So this is what the Pied Piper felt like," he whispered to Becky.

They'd barely set foot in the parlor when his solace vanished as Mary wailed in pain.

TEN

Fifteen minutes and a dozen shrieks later, Emma came out of Mary's room, sleeves rolled up and looking frazzled. "I know it's a lot to ask," she whispered to Nate, "but I don't want the children to hear any more of this. They've been exposed to so much pain and violence already."

"I'll take them back to your place," he offered. "It'll be suppertime soon. I'll feed them and put them to bed if you're not back by then."

"Thank you, Nate," she sighed, a hand on his arm. "Now I don't want you to worry. It sounds far worse than it is, believe me. It's just that she's such a little thing, and I can tell it's going to be a big, strapping baby."

"You're sure that's all it is?"

"Well, there are no guarantees in life, but as I said, she's healthy and strong."

She was saying all the right things, but Nate saw the fear glimmering in Emma's eyes. He drew her into a comforting embrace. "She couldn't be in more capable hands," he said reassuringly. And holding her at arm's length, he looked her square in the eye. "God and all His angels will be right there with you. I'll be prayin' for it."

Emma nodded. "I'll just say a word to the children before you leave."

"And I'll have a word with Mary while you do."

Nate walked quietly into his sister-in-law's room and knelt beside the bed. She looked so small and fragile, lying there beneath the covers. He took her tiny hand in his and kissed the knuckles.

Mary lifted a corner of the neatly folded compress that covered her eyes and grinned. "I thought you were mindin' the children," she said weakly.

"Aye. That I was. But they're hungry, the lot of 'em, so I'm takin' 'em back to Emma's to put some food in their bellies."

She dropped the cloth back into place and sighed. "I'm sorry that my caterwaulin' is frightenin' the little tikes. I'm tryin' to be brave, really I am. But the pain is like nothin' I've ever felt before." She squeezed his hand hard. "I'm scared, Nate. What if..."

"Hush," he said when her voice trailed off. "Just lie there and rest. You're gonna need your strength." He patted her hand. "Why, you should've heard Suisan when her babies were born. It's a miracle she didn't shake the shingles from the roof!"

"She carried on, too, then?"

The fact of the matter was that Suisan had barely uttered a sound through three deliveries. Though no bigger than Mary, his stoic older sister seemed determined to have her babies the way she did everything else, and she grit her teeth and set her mind to getting through the pain as quickly and efficiently as possible. But if thinking Suisan hollered up a storm calmed Mary, it was a fib Nate was willing to tell. "Why, folks could hear her a mile away!"

She smiled a bit at that. "Go on with you now," she whispered. "Now get on with you; I feel another pain comin', and I don't want to scare the children again."

Nate pressed a kiss to her cheek. "Next time I see you, you'll be the mother of my brother's firstborn. I'm proud of you, Mary O'Neil."

He closed her door behind him. "There's another pain on its way," he told Emma. "She needs you."

Nodding, she put her hand on the doorknob. "I've told Ian he should come with you...that Mary's suffering more than she needs to because worrying about him is making her tense." She glanced in Ian's direction. "But he won't listen to reason. Will you talk some sense into him?"

Nate followed her gaze to his pacing brother's worried face. "Seems he's already doin' the sensible thing. Mary's his wife, and that's his baby she's havin'. This is where he belongs, Emma. It's where I'd be if..." *If it were you in there havin' my baby,* he thought. But Nate couldn't allow himself to speak the thought aloud. Indeed, he had no business thinking such a thing in the first place. Instead, he said, "Sure, he's scared and worried; that's natural and normal, too, isn't it?"

Emma smiled. "I suppose you're right. Give us 'til supper-time, then send Matthew down to see how we're doing. Maybe by then, you'll have another niece or nephew to spoil rotten!"

He yearned to draw her near and kiss away the fear on her beautiful face. It took every ounce of strength in him to walk to the door.

Remembering how well the children responded to her teasing game before dinner last week, he called out, "Last one to Emma's is a rotten egg!"

Their exuberant peals of laughter and squeals of delight drowned out Mary's moans. As he jogged along behind the children, he recalled the verse from Revelations: *"And she being with child cried, travailing in birth, and pained to be delivered..."*

"God be with her and keep her safe," he prayed, "for this world would be a dismal place without Mary."

⌒

It had taken nearly a full day for little Liam O'Neil to be born.

Little, indeed, Nate grinned when Ian told him the baby weighed nearly ten pounds. "Why, Mary's not a hundred pounds soaking wet," he said, slapping the proud papa on the back. "Your boy's barely a day old, and already he's a tenth the size of his ma!"

And when he heard how Emma's calm demeanor was the thing that kept Mary from straining to the point where she might bleed to death, Nate's heart swelled with love and pride for her. More than ever, he realized how undeserving he was of such a woman.

"So tell me, big brother, when are you goin' to ask Emma to be your bride?"

The older children were outside playing, and Becky was napping as the brothers sat at Emma's table, sipping coffee and enjoying the quiet of the morning.

"Never, that's when."

"Are you daft, man? She blushes like a bride whenever you're around. And as for you, you're so stuck on her, you're downright sticky!"

Nate leaned back in his chair and frowned. "It's too complicated to explain. There's more to this than what meets the eye."

Ian's dark brows drew together as he aimed a powerful forefinger at his brother. "Don't be talkin' to me like I'm some simpleton," he growled. "If there's more to it than meets the eye, then spell it out, here and now. How else am I goin' to help you?"

He heaved a huge, sad sigh. "You can't help me, Ian."

"You won't let me help, y'mean."

Hanging his head, Nate blew a stream of air past his lips. "She deserves a better man than me. That's all there is to it."

"A better man!" Ian slammed a fist onto the tabletop, rattling the cups and saucers and spoons. "Why, there's only one man better, and much as it pains me to say it, I'm already spoken for."

The brothers locked eyes, and Ian's hearty guffaws mingled with Nate's halfhearted laughter. "No brag, just fact, eh, brother?"

"You've got it!" Ian's smile dimmed. "I can't tell you how it feels to wake up beside Mary. Why, the poets haven't begun to describe what's in my heart when I look at her sleeping face. And now that she's given me a child…."

Though he smiled from ear to ear, Ian's eyes welled with tears. "Mary's my whole world, Nate. She's the reason I get out of bed every mornin'…and the reason I get in every evenin'," he added with a sly wink. Grinning, Ian flexed his biceps. "She makes me feel strong as an ox, smart as a wizard, more handsome than any actor on the stage."

Leaning forward, Ian grinned impishly. "Sittin' here now, I can admit that I'm none of those things. But Mary…" He shook his head at the wonderment of it. "Mary believes I'm all that and more!"

His voice grew softer when he added, "It's a glorious thing, big brother, to have a woman feel that way about you. Makes a man feel he could take on the whole English army single-handed, and win!"

"I'm happy for you, Ian. Truly I am. But you earned your life by livin' it straight and true." He frowned. "I can't have what you have, 'cause I haven't earned it; 'cause I've done things I can never make up for."

Furrowing his brow in disbelief, Ian tucked in one side of his mouth. "You're talkin' nonsense. What things have you done?"

Nate had never told a soul about that night on the battlefield. Could he confess the sin to his younger brother, and risk losing his respect?

"I had a battle with the whiskey," he began.

"Aye. That's no secret," Ian injected.

"It caused me to do things, wicked things."

Chuckling, Ian said, "What. Did you kiss a saloon girl? Even God would forgive you those transgressions."

"I killed a hundred men." There. The truth was out. Now let the dust settle where it may.

Ian lifted one brow and grinned. "With your bare hands, or with a cutlass?"

Nate scowled. "I'm serious, Ian! I'm responsible for the deaths of nearly a hundred of my fellow soldiers!"

His brother's grin faded. "That's impossible. No man could kill that many...."

Nate almost heard Ian's unspoken *"unless...."*

"He could if he got drunk on his watch, and let the enemy ride roughshod over the camp."

"How much whiskey did you drink?"

Nate shrugged, remembering how that offered bottle had been nearly empty when he'd drained it. "A couple of swigs. What difference does that make?"

Ian turned his face away, unable to look into his brother's shocked eyes a moment longer.

"You're a big, strappin' man, Nathan O'Neil. I've seen you gulp down more of the dog that bit you than any man in three counties, and leave the pub of your own steam." He shook his head violently. "You can't convince me that a few swallows knocked you so cold the Yanks could sneak up on you. Nope. There's more to the story, I'm sure of it." He thought a moment. "Where'd you get the whiskey?"

Hank Campbell had given it to him. "From another soldier. Why?"

"Then he's at the bottom of it. I'd stake my life on it."

Nate's heart thumped with affection for his brother. "God love you, Ian O'Neil, for forgivin' even me most horrible sins. But the terrible fact is, what I'm sayin' is true. I got drunk, and fell asleep on my watch, and when I woke up, all my comrades were dead or dyin'."

Ian narrowed one eye. "All of 'em?"

"All but Campbell."

"Not Hank Campbell, who's been loiterin' around town these past few weeks," Ian interrupted.

"One and the same."

"I don't like the man, Nate. Don't ask me why. It's his eyes, I think, that give me the feelin' he's up to no good all the time. It's as though every minute of the day, he's busy thinkin' up ways to hoodwink folks or worse."

"I don't like him, either. But..." From time to time, he'd wondered if Campbell had added something to that whiskey bottle, but he'd shrugged it off. For one thing, he couldn't explain to himself what Campbell would have gained by doing something so dastardly. For another, blaming someone else for his own dastardly deed only added to his misery.

"But nothing! You were wounded in that battle; what happened to Campbell?"

Nate stroked his beard. "Didn't have a scratch on him."

"And how do you explain that, when the rest of the men were dead or dyin' when you woke up, bleedin' from a dozen places? He put somethin' in that bottle, Nate. I'd stake my son's life on it!"

"Don't talk nonsense, Ian," Nate scolded. "What reason would Campbell have to spike my whiskey?"

"Maybe he was a double agent. Men are capable of some despicable acts when the price is right."

"You're readin' too many of those dime Westerns, little brother," Nate said, smiling despite himself, "and the fiction has addled your brain. Hank Campbell is guilty of something, I'll grant you, but a double agent?"

"He's got the brains for it. I've had a conversation or two with him. Did you know he has a college degree?"

"He does not."

"Yes, he does. Told me so himself. And from the high-falootin' way he speaks, I have to believe it's true."

Nate pondered Ian's suggestions. "He does talk awful fancy-like, doesn't he?"

"Makes you wonder why a college man weren't an officer. And why he spends so much time with old Doc Farley. The two of 'em were drunk as skunks the other day in the barber shop, and got to talkin' about the war...Farley braggin' that he earned two pay-checks every month workin' both sides of the Mason-Dixon line, and Campbell actin' like it weren't news to him."

"Farley? A double agent? Now *that* I believe, but Campbell?"

Ian only nodded. "And did you know the pair of 'em served together in Gettysburg?"

He shook his head. "I don't know."

"Don't you see, Nathan? Farley had access to any kind of drug he wanted. If he and Campbell were workin' together...."

"You're lookin' for a convenient scapegoat to blame my frailties on, Ian. And much as I love you for it, I can't let you go on foolin' yourself. I'm the lout who caused a hundred deaths, nobody else."

"I don't believe it for a minute. I dismissed all their drunken talk as nonsense...'til now. But if Farley and Campbell had a partnership...."

Despite his protestations, Nate had hope for the first time in years. Hope that he wasn't the deviate he believed himself to be. Hope that he could sleep at night, and not fear the horrible, haunting nightmares. Hope that he might share his life with Emma.

But even if what Ian said was true, it couldn't be proven. Or could it?

⌣

"Twenty dollars a month?" Matt echoed. "Why, I know some grown men who don't make that much!"

"I'll tack on an extra five for every other boy and girl you can talk into coming along."

He watched Matthew ciphering his would-be salary. The boy's brow furrowed when he said, "I'd like to go, Hank, really I would, but I never learned to ride a horse."

Campbell ignored the fear glimmering in the boy's eyes. "Born and bred on a farm, and you can't ride? I don't believe it," he taunted.

"Well…Emma doesn't want me goin' near 'em." He hesitated, ground the toe of his boot into the dirt. "She's been scared of horses, ever since…."

Campbell knew only too well what had happened to Matt's family that awful day in September. But he needed to prod the boy on, if he was to accomplish his goal. "Emma is afraid of horses?" Campbell frowned. "I understand, son. Big animal like that can be scary to a grown man, let alone a little boy like you."

Matt stood taller and squared his chin. "Little boy? I ain't no little boy. I ain't scared of horses, neither!" Nervously, he glanced in the direction of Campbell's big black steed. "And I'll prove it, if you'll let me borrow your horse."

Campbell bit back a satisfied smirk. His plan was unfolding… like five crisp hundred dollar bills.

"I don't know, Matt, Diablo is awfully feisty."

The boy glanced at the animal, blinking and swallowing as it bobbed its huge head and nervously pawed the dirt. "I can do it," he insisted, his voice trembling slightly.

Campbell shrugged. "Alright. If you say so," he said, handing the reins to Matt.

The boy's hands shook as he grasped the worn leather. His face blanched and perspiration dotted his forehead. But he pressed on, gritting his teeth determinedly as he shoved his hoot into the stirrup.

"Need a hand up, son?"

"No sir," Matt said, breathlessly.

He could see Matt's sweaty handprint on the back of the saddle and feel the boy's palpable fear. And yet Matt swung himself into the saddle. He sat up, staring straight ahead, fighting his fear with every ounce of courage he could muster. It almost made Campbell admire his pluck. "Come on down from there, son," he said. "You've showed me your mettle."

But Matt, stoic as before, tightened his grip on the saddle horn. "Cowboy has to sit a saddle."

Campbell reached up and hoisted the boy down. "You did fine, Matthew. Just fine," he said. And he meant it.

But Matthew seemed unable to hear the compliment, and hung his head, and Campbell's admiration grew. "If need be, you can ride behind me."

"You don't need a coward like me comin' along on a cattle drive."

"You're no coward," he said, meaning it. "I'd be right proud to have a man like you along on the trail, Matt." He extended his hand.

But Matt was too busy staring at the ground to see it.

"You know Miss Emma needs that money, son."

Matt took a deep breath. "I know," he said, letting it out again. "And I want to help her. I just don't know if I can do it."

"'Course you can do it. Man can do anything for a woman who needs him." He waited a moment, to give the idea time to penetrate Matt's terror-struck mind. "So, do we have a deal?"

The boy looked at Campbell's hand, tightened his own into a fist. Then he met the man's eyes. For an instant, Campbell felt certain Matthew could read his mind, for a glint of self-loathing shimmered in his blue orbs.

"I guess," Matthew answered. And he walked off, slump-shouldered and dragging his feet as the man grimaced at what he'd done. *And I am proud of you, Matthew, getting up on that horse after what you've been through.* He grimaced. *Ain't so proud of me, though....*

Well, now, he said to himself, *what're you going to do with the money you're taking to torture this young'un?* He rolled the thought around in his head a time or two. *First thing you'll buy is a steaming hot bath, 'cause right now, Hank Campbell, you stink to high heaven.*

⸻

It seemed that every time she rounded a corner, she heard the children whispering. And almost without exception, the moment she entered a room, the whispering abruptly stopped and all five of the older children sat, somber and silent and staring straight ahead like stone statues. Emma shared her concerns with Mary when she stopped by to examine the new mother and her baby.

"They're no doubt playin' some secret game," Mary said, smiling. "I'm the youngest of twelve children, y'see, so I remember plenty of secret games. 'Twas more a rarity when my brothers and sisters didn't have some sort of conspiracy goin' on behind me parents backs."

"But what if they're up to something dangerous? What if their game harms them in some way?"

Mary shrugged. "Don't be such a worrywart, Emma! How badly can they get hurt, playin' children's games? If they scrape their knees or get splinters in their fingers, you're a nurse, by God's grace. You'll bandage their boo-boos and scold 'em soundly, and send 'em to bed without their supper so they'll learn to take better care in the future."

Emma sighed. "I suppose you're right." She grinned at her newest patient. "How did you get so child-smart so fast?"

Blushing with pride, Mary grinned. "I suppose motherin' just comes natural to some of us." She stopped talking when she saw how her comment was received by Emma, whose wide eyes and slack jaw were physical proof that words could sting every bit as much as a hickory switch.

"Oh, darlin' girl," Mary said, squeezing Emma's hands, "y'know I didn't mean that the way it came out. Why, I think you're a splendid mother. So does everyone in town. May God singe me hair with a lightning bolt if I'm not tellin' the truth!"

"Hush, Mary," Emma said, patting her friend's hand. "You'll wake little Liam. Now, how about that cup of tea you promised me?"

The women sat at Mary's kitchen table, chatting quietly about knickknacks and the church social and the new schoolmarm who was scheduled to arrive in the summer. Mary's conversation took an unexpected turn when she said, "So tell me, Emma, when d'you think Nate'll pop the question, soon?"

Emma gasped. "Why, Mary, what a thing to say." Grinning, she shook her head and her forefinger at the same time, and assumed a maternal, scolding tone. "I think you should have had twins..."

It was Mary's turn to gasp.

"...because," Emma finished, "little Liam isn't keeping you nearly busy enough if you've had time to come up with an idea like that!"

Her Irish friend shrugged. "'Tis a perfectly legitimate question. You love him and he loves you. Seems to me the altar is the next logical step."

He loves me? "Really, Mary, Nate has never said or done anything to indicate—"

"If you haven't seen it in his eyes, you haven't been lookin', and if you haven't heard it in his voice, then you haven't been listenin', either. It's plain as the daisies on your frock," she said, pointing to the crocheted flower trim on Emma's collar. "Your 'glamour' is all over him."

"My 'glamour'?"

"Aye. 'Tis an old Irish sayin'. It means your fairy dust is on him...he's smitten with you."

Unconsciously, Emma pressed a hand against her heart. "He's a very sweet man, there's no denying that, but just because..."

"Are you daft, woman? The man would marry you in a heartbeat if he thought you'd say yes!"

For a long moment, she could only stare and blink at Mary. "Has he...did he tell you that?"

"Didn't have to. I've got eyes and ears. I know a love-struck man when I see one." Mary took a sip of her tea, then added, "And you're lookin' mighty moon-eyed yourself, Emma Wright."

"Me! But I..."

"What is it President Lincoln said? 'You can fool some of the people some of the time, but you can't fool all of the people all of the time.' Near as I can tell, it means 'You trick your friends and I'll trick mine, but let's not trick each other.' You're a woman in love, sure as I'm sittin' here. There's no point denyin' the obvious."

Emma chewed her bottom lip. "Is it? Obvious, I mean?"

"Yanks!" Mary sighed, rolling her eyes. "Here on this side of the ocean, you've got all sorts of rules and regulations to keep you honest, yet you go to all manner of trouble to hide from the truth. Yes, it's obvious that you love him. And what's wrong with that!"

Tucking in a corner of her mouth, Emma shook her head. "There's nothing wrong with that," she said softly. "He's a wonderful man. And if he asked me to marry him, I would say yes."

"Why do I hear a 'but' in that sentence?" Mary asked, a suspicious glint in her eyes.

"Because I don't think he'll ask me; that's why." Emma sighed again, shrugging her shoulders. "I'm nearly as tall as he is. A man wants a woman who's..." She searched for the right word.

"...beautiful, inside and out," Mary finished for her, "and who'll make him feel like he hung the moon."

Liam stirred in his cradle, and the women got ready for the hunger cries that would soon follow. "Tell him how you feel, Emma. There's no shame in admittin' that you're in love."

"No...not in admitting it. The shame only comes when you confess your feelings, and find out you've been suffering from delusions. 'Unrequited love,' I think they call it."

"Nate needs you, Emma, and you need him, too. Don't let false pride nor silly fears keep you from havin' what Ian and I have."

"But it seems so forward, so bold!"

"Take the bull by the horns!" Mary stood beside Emma's chair and gave her friend a sideways hug. Nodding toward the cradle, she grinned mischievously. "I did. Need I say more?"

Emma grinned and headed for the door. "Oh, and Mary," she said, heading out, "I wouldn't call an American a 'Yank', not on this side of the Mason-Dixon line. It could get you into trouble!"

Mary had given her a lot to think about, and Emma considered it all through the long, dark night.

Dear Lord, she prayed, *I want to do Your will. I pray Nate is the one You want for me.* She paced the length and breadth of her room, elbows cupped in her palms, staring at the polished wood planks beneath her feet.

One of these days—hopefully not too soon—all of the children would have found loving homes, except for Jenni. Eventually, even she'd leave to start a family of her own. *And what will you have then, Emma, save the memories of a love that could have been?*

Show me the way, Lord. She opened her Bible to the book of Psalms, and read silently. "*I delight to do thy will, O my God: yea thy law is within my heart…Teach me to do thy will; for thou art my God: thy spirit is good; lead me into the land of uprightness.*" With His promise firm in her mind, Emma felt the first stirrings of sleepiness. She went from room to room, checking on the children once more before turning in.

Marcie slept fitfully, and always kicked her covers off. Emma draped the girl with the soft plaid blanket, then kissed her smooth brow.

Jenni, as always, slept on her left side, a pillow scrunched against her chest. Emma brushed a strand of flaxen hair from the girl's forehead, and kissed the tip of her nose.

Stevie liked to cuddle up to his big brother, and Ryan didn't seem to mind a bit that the boy sometimes sprawled spread-eagle, like a bony blanket. She adjusted their covers as best she could without waking them, and gave each a light kiss on the cheek.

Matthew, flat on his stomach, would have died of embarrassment to know that he sucked his thumb as he slept. She pulled the offending digit from his mouth and gave him a quick peck on the ear.

And little Becky, snoozing contentedly in her cradle at the foot of Emma's bed, sucked an imaginary bottle. *What are you dreaming, little one?* Emma wondered, watching her angelic face twitch and grin as she slept. *Are you thinking of the day when you'll sit up all by yourself and crawl from here to there, and toddle across the parlor?* She tidied the baby's blankets. *I, for one, am in no hurry to see you stand on your own, for that's when you'll begin walking away from me.*

Yawning deeply, Emma slipped beneath her covers and closed her eyes. She reached out and stroked the empty pillow beside hers.

"Oh, Nate," Emma whispered wistfully as she drifted off to sleep. And feeling very much like a young girl experiencing her first love, she sighed, "I'd be so proud and so happy to learn it's true...that you really love me."

ELEVEN

Pacing back and forth on the path where he told the children to meet him, Campbell checked his pocket watch. They were ten minutes late. Had they changed their minds?

It wouldn't surprise him if they had. Thanks to the dream he had about Emma, Campbell almost backed out of the deal himself. His sleeping mind transported him several years into the future, and he was able to watch himself enter Emma's house.

Drying her hands on a ruffled apron, she greeted him with a warm smile and kiss. "Wash up for supper," she said, shooing him toward the pump, "I've made your favorite...roasted chicken and mashed potatoes."

The baby in the cradle was not one of Emma's orphans. His name was Hank Campbell, Junior. And the beautiful little girl who danced into the room, blond braids bouncing and blue eyes flashing with welcome, was his daughter.

"Did you have a hard day at work, Daddy?" she asked, hugging his knees.

Scooping her into his arms, he kissed her round rosy cheek. "None of my days are hard. Not when I have all of you to come home to."

He sat on the edge of his hotel mattress for nearly an hour, reviewing the dream. He'd never lived in one place longer than a year. Growing roots, he contended, was the most uncomfortable feeling a man could experience. But if he could believe his dream was possible, he would grow roots all the way to China and back!

Campbell could count on one hand the number of times he'd been alone with Emma. And despite his college education, he doubted he could count high enough to add up the number of times he thought about her in his private moments.

O'Neil was right...there wasn't a man around good enough for the likes of Emma Wright. She gave of herself like no woman he ever knew...would ever know. Though he sensed his "Emma" dream would never come true, the possibility that it might gave him pause. The way she looked at him, with those clear, innocent blue eyes of hers, made him feel whole and clean and good, something he hadn't felt since...

Campbell couldn't remember when he last felt like a decent human being. He would gladly settle for nothing more than her friendship, just to have an occasional opportunity to be around her, bathing his dreary soul in the kindness and warmth that poured from her like water from a fountain.

If she ever found out about his part in Farley's plan for her children, he would consider himself fortunate if she ever so much as looked in his direction again.

That fear is what made Campbell consider backing out on the deal with Farley. But he splashed cold water on his face, and drank two piping hot cups of strong black coffee, and filled his belly with ham and eggs and buttered bread, and came to his senses.

A woman like Emma Wright could never be his. Not even in friendship. *So why turn your back on five hundred dollars, regardless of how it was earned?* he asked himself.

So he'd saddled his horse, packed up his saddle bags, loaded his shotgun, and headed for the path where the children were to meet him at four o'clock in the morning.

Campbell searched the horizon for a sign of them. The crimson and golden streaks coloring the deep purple of the morning sky told him it would be a warm, clear day, a good day for traveling. Setting his jaw with grim determination, he inhaled sharply. *A good day for putting this town…and everyone in it…behind you,* he told himself.

⌒

Becky's gurgles and coos woke Emma gently. Smiling, she stretched languorously. "You're awfully chipper this morning," she told the baby. "A full night's sleep seems to agree with you."

Emma climbed out of bed and slipped into her chenille robe. Bundling Becky into her arms, she drizzled kisses over the giggling child's chubby cheeks. Standing at the window, she parted the curtains. "Why did you let me sleep so late? Do you know the last time I slept 'til seven?"

The baby blinked in response.

"I'll tell you when. I haven't stayed in bed past five since I was twelve years old and came down with a case of the measles!"

Becky bounced up and down, excited by the sight of horse-drawn wagons and carts passing to and fro in the street below. "Isn't it a beautiful day, Becky? Maybe later, I'll pop you into your tram and take you for a nice long walk. What do you think of that?"

Becky's toothless grin settled it. "No 'maybes' about it. Today, we're going to strut down Main Street and show you off. Now, let's get your brothers and sisters up and feed them some breakfast."

"Matthew," she called as she headed for the boys' room. "Ryan, Steven. Up and at 'em, boys, or you'll be late for school."

Their beds were made up, and the window shade pulled up. "Well, now," Emma whispered to the baby, "where do you suppose those mischief-makers are so early in the morning? Let's see if the girls know what's going on."

She found the same fastidiousness in the girls' room. Grinning with glee, she raced down the stairs. Once or twice, they got up before her, and started breakfast to surprise her. But only on Saturday mornings, when no one was in a rush to get to school or church on time. The kitchen was as neat and quiet as the children's rooms.

Emma yanked open the back door and poked her head outside. "Matthew!" she hollered. "Jenni?"

No answer.

"Matthew!" she shouted, more loudly this time. "Jenni!" Silence.

Unaccustomed to so much yelling, little Becky's lower lip quivered and she began to cry. "Oh, I'm sorry little one. I didn't mean to frighten you." She closed the door and turned in one slow circle, frowning as she considered all the places the children might be.

And then she saw it, propped against the salt and pepper shakers in the middle of the kitchen table. *Dear Emma*, said the first, bold line, printed in Matthew's now-familiar strong hand. Tucking Becky into the high chair, she sat at the table and, with trembling hands, grabbed the note.

Dear Emma,

We have gone off to earn us some money, our Mother's Day surprise for you. Don't worry about us. We will be just fine. Hank says he will take good care of us. There is just one week of school left, so don't worry about that, either.

I made sure everyone packed plenty of clean shirts and socks, and their hats and mittens, too, in case nights on the trail are cold.

Emma gasped and squeezed her eyes shut. Had she read correctly? What did Matt mean..."on the trail"? What kind of nonsensical boyhood game was he playing this time? Taking a deep breath, she finished reading:

> *Hank says it will take us two weeks to get to Nebraska, and three weeks after that, we should be back in Ellicott City with Mister Zaph's herd of cattle. Now you won't have to worry how you'll pay for our school shoes, because Hank says he's going to pay us each twenty whole dollars.*
>
> *I packed my school tablet and three pencils. If there is time, I will write you again. Jenni and Ryan and Stevie said to tell you they love you, and Marcie says she misses you already. The same goes for me, of course.*
>
> *Affectionately yours,*
> *Matthew Evans Wright*

Emma's heart thundered. Hank Campbell took her children on a cattle drive, without her knowledge or permission? Whatever was wrong with the man!?

"They couldn't have much of a head start," she whispered, looking at the carriage clock above the stove. "It's barely past seven. Maybe, if we hurry, we can catch them."

Lifting Becky from the high chair, she raced up the stairs. "Wait right there," she said, putting the baby back into the cradle, "while I get dressed." Emma tore off her nightgown, and slipped a petticoat over her head. Quickly, she stepped into a full black skirt, and tucked a plain white blouse into its waistband. Sitting on the edge of the bed, she pulled on black stockings and her low-heeled black boots. And without even bothering to glance in the mirror, she knotted her long hair into an untidy bun.

"Come on, Becky," she said, grabbing the infant from the cradle. "Let's find Mr. Nate. Maybe he has a couple of fast horses he'll let us borrow."

⌒

The boys led the way, riding side by side, with the girls close on their heels. Campbell changed position every fifteen minutes or so, first riding out to see what lay ahead, then closing the ranks to watch their backs.

"I'm tired," Stevie complained. "And this saddle is hurting my…"

"Oh, stop your whining," Matthew scolded in a hoarse whisper. "You don't want Hank to take us home, do you?"

Pouting, Stevie nodded. "Yes. I want to go home. I miss Emma."

"Well, you can't have her," Ryan injected, "because she's all the way back in Ellicott City, and we're…" He looked left and right, then straight ahead. "Where do you suppose we are?" he asked Matt.

Matt rolled his eyes. "We've only been riding for a couple of hours. We couldn't have gone more than ten miles, slow as we're moving."

"I'm hungry," Stevie whimpered. "And the saddle is…"

"We know," Ryan interrupted, "it's hurting your…"

"If the two of you don't quit it, I'm going to…" Matt frowned and shook a fist in the brothers' direction. "I don't know what I'm going to do, but I can tell you this…you aren't going to like it!"

"Be patient with Stevie," Jenni said from behind them. "He's just a little boy."

"He's not a little boy," Ryan snarled, "he's a little baby. We should have left him at Emma's, with Becky, the other little baby."

"I'm not a baby!" Stevie protested. "I'm big enough. Hank even said so!"

He was trailing behind them, listening to their bickering for miles now, and frankly, didn't know how much more of it he could stand. Hank scrubbed a leather-gloved hand over his face and took a deep breath, hoping the actions would produce the patience required to endure another two weeks of this nonsense.

"If you're big enough, then you'll stop crying about what that saddle is doing to your..."

"I'm not crying," Stevie insisted. "I'm talking, is all."

That does it! Campbell thought, spurring his horse ahead until she trotted alongside Matthew's mare. "Stop talking," he said to Stevie. And when the boy's eyes widened with fright at his angry tone, Campbell exhaled in exasperation. "I'll tell you what. I'll pay a dollar to the one of you who's quietest from here on out."

Matthew grinned. "A dollar a day? A dollar a mile? A dollar a what?" he wanted to know.

No doubt about it, Hank liked this boy. *Reminds me of myself at his age,* Campbell thought, grinning right back at him. "I'm going to keep count of every word each of you speaks, starting right now," he said, taking a small notebook and a stubby pencil from his shirt pocket. "When we lay down to bed for the night, whoever was quietest gets the silver dollar."

"Whoever was quietest, or whoever talked the least?" Matt asked, his eyes glinting with mischief. "'Cause I can be quiet as a church mouse when I want to be..."

Chuckling, Campbell aimed a forefinger at the boy. "Both," he answered, quirking a brow. He slid a shiny silver dollar from his pocket and held it between his thumb and forefinger and, looking at each child in turn, added, "Think it's worth it?"

The girls only rolled their eyes, but all three boys nodded eagerly. Campbell re-pocketed the coin and urged his horse forward. "I'm going to ride up ahead for a bit, check out the lay of the land. Matthew, I'm putting you in charge. Keep all these young'uns together, now, and whatever you do, don't let that pack mule out of your sight. She's carrying our tents and vittles...things that have to last us until we get to Nebraska."

"To Nebraska?" Marcie asked. "But what about the trip home? Is there enough food to get us back to Ellicott City again?"

This bunch is smarter than I gave 'em credit for, Campbell acknowledged. "No sense loading old Bessie down that a-way," he explained. "We'll buy what we need at the other end of the trail. Now, y'all behave yourselves and do what Matthew tells you, y'hear? Stay close together, and don't get off the trail. I won't be long."

Farley is out of his mind if he thinks I'm taking a measly five hundred for this job. I never imagined being a nursemaid would be so much bother. Why, I oughta demand five hundred for each kid, plus expenses!

Campbell decided to discuss his pay with the doctor first thing after returning to Ellicott City. *If you can't make Farley see reason,* he told himself, shrugging nonchalantly, *you'll just keep all the money you're to collect from the ranchers.* He might just do that, anyway, and not bother going back to Maryland at all.

As he told Farley, he'd done some pretty despicable things in his day, some just for fun, but mostly, for the money. He couldn't remember a time when a job caused him so much as a tweak of conscience. Even looking into the grief-stricken faces of folks he fleeced hadn't stolen a minute of his sleep. Guilt was an emotion he simply couldn't afford if he hoped to stay in this line of work. And since it was easier than honest work....

He'd been a crook and a con man all his adult life, but, as he liked to tell prospective employers, at least he'd been an honorable thief, delivering whatever he promised to deliver, without ever having double-crossed a boss.

Until now.

Even he didn't understand why the idea of going back to Ellicott City tied his gut in a knot. But Campbell couldn't explain something he never experienced before, now could he?

If he took a moment to be honest with himself, he would have to admit neither Farley nor the money had anything to do with his plan to stay in Nebraska after delivering the children.

Emma Wright was the one and only reason he wanted to avoid that town. Because facing her—even from a distance after what he'd done to her children—would be the toughest thing he'd ever do in his life.

⌒

She stood in the double-wide doorway to Nate's warehouse, wringing a lace hanky in her trembling hands. He'd never seen her looking so distraught. Not when Becky's fever spiked dangerously high. Not when Marcie nearly cut her own finger off slicing a beef roast. Not even in the aftermath of the accident that made Matthew an orphan.

She handled Mary's difficult delivery with the precision of a skilled surgeon. And somehow, she kept Ian calm all through the long hours of his wife's hard labor. Something horrible must have happened to put tears and panic in her eyes.

He went to her immediately, and she melted into his arms. "Oh, Nate," she whispered, "they're gone."

"Who's gone?" he asked, lovingly stroking her hair.

"The children. Except for Becky, they're all gone."

He held her at arm's length. "Whatever are you talkin' about, Emma?"

She dabbed at her eyes with a corner of the hanky. "I overslept this morning, and when I went in to wake them for school…" Emma bit her lower lip in an effort to stay in control. "They were… they were gone."

"But sure they couldn't have gone far. Did you check the river? You know how those boys love fishin'. Maybe they talked the girls into goin' along."

Reaching into a side pocket in her skirt, Emma withdrew a slip of paper. "They left this," she said, handing it to him.

He didn't want to let her go, not even long enough to read the note. Nate led her farther into the warehouse, and helped her sit on a bale of hay against the wall. "Where's the baby?"

"Mary's watching her," she said. And, impatient for him to read the note, Emma shook his wrist. "I already checked with Mr. Zaph. He never even heard of him, so they aren't going west to bring back a herd of cattle for him. Oh, Nate, what do you make of it? Why would he take them? Could he really do anything so underhanded, so despicable?"

He almost asked who "he" was, but thought better of it. Once he read the note, he would understand…he hoped.

When he finished, Nate met her red-rimmed eyes. Much as he wanted to comfort and console Emma, he wanted to get his hands on Campbell even more. He stood and began pacing, punching one work-hardened fist into his other palm. "You say you talked to Zaph? And he didn't send Campbell west for cows?"

Emma shook her head. "He's investing everything in dairy cows. He got the first ones from Pennsylvania."

"Why, that no-good, rotten, stinking polecat. I'll cut his heart out and feed it to him for supper!"

He stopped his furious pacing, but only because Emma blocked his path. "He can't have gone very far," she said "not with five young children in tow. I'm sure if we leave right now, and ride hard, we can catch up with them."

The sight of her tear-streaked face struck a tender choir inside him, and cooled his hot rage. Hands on her shoulder he said in a soft voice, "But Emma, m'darlin', we don't even know which way they've gone."

She poked at the note in his hands. "It says something about a ranch in Nebraska. There's only one decent road going west out of town. Surely he took it."

Nate felt the rage building again as he pictured the man, smug and arrogant in his buckskins and boots. What Ian had said about Campbell and Farley being in cahoots gonged in his mind. Did their so-called partnership have anything to do with the disappearance of the children? Nate intended to find out, and when he did...

"Campbell is too smart for that. Knowin' we'll be after him like a fox after chickens, he'll take some seldom-used trail."

"Mountain Run!" she said, starting up a pacing trail of her own. "It hasn't been used for anything but logging since before the war. It would be overgrown by now, and..."

"...And nearly impossible to track him," Nate nodded, following her meaning. "That'd be his style, all right."

He half-ran to the back of the shop. "Tell Sheriff Carter where I've gone," he said, throwing a soft blanket over his white mare's back. "Ask him to round up a search party."

She put her hands on her hips. "Tell him yourself."

"What?" Nate asked distractedly as he cinched the saddle.

"You tell the sheriff to round up a search party," she said as he flung open a cabinet door. Emma watched him take a pistol from a shelf with one hand, and lift the lid from a box of shells with the other. One by one, he slid bullets into the chamber and snapped it shut. Engaging the safety, he dropped the gun into his saddlebag.

"All right, then. I'll tell him on my way out of town. Come," he said, draping an arm over her shoulders, "walk with me to the door." Once there, he slid one boot into a stirrup. "Well, I'm on my way," he said, preparing to hoist himself into the saddle.

"You're not going anywhere without me." And as if to prove it, she grabbed hold of his horse's reins.

Both feet on solid ground again, he attempted to talk sense to her. "I understand why you're upset, Emma, and I don't blame you a bit. But I can travel faster alone."

She lifted her chin determinedly. "You don't know how to find the trail. I can show you. It'll save time. You know I'm right," she said, matter-of-factly. "Now, do you have a saddle for that beast?" she asked, pointing to the black steed in the next stall.

"I do."

He could see there was no point in arguing with her. "But I think it's only fair to tell you a thing or two about me before we set out," Nate said, guiding her back to the hay bale.

It spilled out fast and furious, a fact that surprised him, considering the only other person he ever told the story to was his brother. Perhaps, Nate considered, it had been good to practice on Ian before telling Emma.

When he finished, he sat beside her, elbows balanced on his knees, head hanging in shame as he waited for her to say something, anything, to end the terrible silence that punctuated his story.

Finally, Emma said, "If there's a word of truth to your tale... and I don't believe for a minute that there is...it's in the missing piece to the puzzle."

"Missing piece? I don't..."

Facing him head-on, she said, "You've left something out, or something else happened that you don't know about, because a man like you couldn't possibly have let a thing like that happen."

*A man like me...*Nate scratched his head. He didn't know what her reaction to his confession might be. Certainly not a sweet sideways hug and a kiss on the cheek!

Emma stood and crossed both arms over her chest. "Now, are you going to saddle that horse, or am I?"

TWELVE

Campbell must have been expecting them, for he sat cross-legged on the ground, both hands in the air in silent surrender. "Keep your voices down," he whispered hoarsely. "No need to wake the young'uns. They've had a long, hard day."

Emma and Nate exchanged puzzled glances, then dismounted their horses and faced him.

"There's a rope in my saddlebag," he said matter-of-factly. "You can use it to hog-tie me."

Nate frowned suspiciously and kept his gun trained on Campbell. "You've taken all the fun out of this for me. I was lookin' forward to puttin' a bullet through your cold, hard heart."

Campbell shrugged. "Can't say I blame you." He nodded toward his own handgun, lying in the dust beside his saddlebag. "Gave a thought or two to saving you the trouble." And shaking his head, he added, "Couldn't leave the young'uns out here to fend for themselves."

More to himself than Emma or Nate, he said, "Before today, I always wondered what folks wanted with young'uns, anyway.

Seemed to me they were nothing but work, worry, and expense."
He glanced at the children, sleeping sound and snug in their bedrolls a short distance away. "They bring out a man's protective side;
make him feel responsible for their every need." He met Emma's
eyes. "I never would have guessed those could be pleasant feelings."

She got onto her knees in front of him. "Why did you do it,
Hank? Why did you take them?" Raising a skeptical brow, she
aimed a forefinger at him. "You may as well tell the truth," she
warned, her voice uncharacteristically hard, "because the sheriff is
hot on our heels, and he knows as well as we do there was no cattle
drive."

Hands still in the air, Campbell calmly nodded. "The cattle
drive was a ruse, all right. I figured the young'uns would feel they
were experiencing an adventure, like in those stories Matt is so
fond of." He looked away, wincing. "Worked like a charm."

Emma got up to inspect the children, stooping now and then
to straighten a blanket or tuck in a tiny hand. "But why, Hank?
Help me understand."

When Campbell lowered his hands, Nate took a step forward,
glowering. "Go ahead, shoot if you want," he growled, rubbing his
biceps.

She read the hot rage glowing in Nate's eyes and, worried he
might just take Campbell up on his invitation, stepped between
the men. "There's time enough for that," Emma said, shooting
Campbell an angry look of her own. "Right now I want to hear his
explanation."

Nate's sarcastic chuckle hung in the chill air like dusty cobwebs. "You don't really expect the truth from a man who'd kidnap
a passel of helpless children, do you?"

She looked from Nate's face to Campbell's and back again.
"There's no logic behind it, I know," she admitted, reading
Campbell's eyes, "but yes, I believe he's going to tell us the truth,

the whole truth and nothing but." Quirking a brow, she challenged him "Aren't you, Hank?"

Scrubbing both hands over his face and lifting the blue-speck-led mug near his knee, he nodded. "I reckon I owe you that, at least." After a long swallow of coffee, he began. When he was finished, he took a deep, shuddering breath, and let it all out slowly.

"You aimed to sell 'em," Nate demanded, his free hand clenching and unclenching at his side, "like...livestock?"

Campbell's dark brows drew together in a scowl. "Farley offered five hundred dollars for the job." Focusing on the liquid in his mug, he shook his head. "I owed some people, and my ma and pa's farm is about to go under. I thought...."

Nate remembered thinking that because Campbell's face was too easy to read, he couldn't possibly be any good at cards. "Gamblin' debts?" he asked.

Eyes still downcast, Campbell nodded.

And so did Nate. "Maybe now I'll shoot you," he snarled.

Campbell only shrugged and tucked in one corner of his mouth in resignation. "I've made my peace with God." And holding both arms parallel to the ground he said, "Man's got to do what a man's got to do."

Nate drove a hand through his hair...and uncocked the gun. "Can't do that. Not unless I shoot myself, too. We're two of a kind, you and me, despicable, dishonorable."

Campbell's puzzled expression slowly faded, and was replaced by a look of understanding and recognition. "If you're talking about that night in Chattanooga," he bit out, "then I have to tell you, we don't have a confounded thing in common."

His heart raced with anticipation. *So Ian was right*, he told himself, taking a step closer. *I can hope he was right, at least.* "I'm listenin', Campbell."

The story spewed from him so fast, Nate wondered why Campbell's breaths didn't blow out the campfire.

"So you've been traipsing around this forsaken country for nearly three years, runnin' from a ghost that didn't exist," he finished on a whisper. "Farley and I killed those soldiers, not you. The doc gave me the powders, and I mixed 'em into your whiskey." His lips thinned with disgust. "Another plan that went like clockwork." Meeting Nate's eyes, he asked, "Want to shoot me now, or at sunup?"

Nate stomped forward, grabbed a handful of Campbell's shirt and brought him to his feet. Nose to nose, he glowered into the man's face. "I ain't gonna shoot you," he growled. "I'm gonna do you a favor, instead."

"A favor?" Campbell asked.

Nate took a step back, cocked a fist, and let it explode against Campbell's jaw, sending the man flying.

Campbell sat sprawled in the dust, grimacing with pain. He shook it off, and grinned as he rubbed his jaw. "Since you call that a favor, I reckon I oughta thank you." He wiped a sleeve across his bloody, already swelling lip.

Nate held out his hand and helped the man up. "Don't mention it," he said.

Emma hid a smile behind one hand, then changed the atmosphere by asking, "You were expecting us, weren't you, Hank?"

Campbell nodded. "Tempting as that money was, I couldn't go through with it. Any man who would make a deal with the likes of Aubrey Farley is as low-down as a man can get...and I oughta know." He hesitated. "God only knows what kind of people they would have ended up with." He hung his head. "I don't think I could have lived with that."

"You may have stirred some pity in Emma's forgivin' soul, but your confessions are only havin' one effect on me." Campbell waited silently for Nate to name that effect.

"You'll be servin' time for what you proposed to do. Hard time, I reckon."

Campbell shrugged one shoulder. "Not hard enough to pay for what I did that night in Tennessee."

Gritting his teeth, Nate shook his head. "Well, you're not alone in that one. I'm as guilty of that crime as you are."

Campbell tucked in his chin in amazement. "How do you figure that? I just told you it was Farley and me who…"

"I believe in givin' credit where credit is due," Nate said quietly. "You drugged my whiskey, but you didn't force me to drink it."

Hard as it was, Nate searched Emma's stern-set face. He wouldn't have blamed her one hit if she'd changed her mind, and now held him accountable for his part in the slaughter.

But Emma said nothing. Instead, she simply stood there, looking lovingly into his eyes. And then she held out her arms, and smiled when he stepped into them.

EPILOGUE

Thanksgiving Day
Fifteen Years Later

Will somebody please pass the mashed potatoes?" Matt asked. "I'm starving!"

"Oh, hush," said his wife. "You'll have Emma and Nate thinking I never feed you!"

"Oh, you needn't worry about that, Annie," Nate said, chuckling, "we can see by the length of his belt that you feed him well!"

"I'll say," Jenni agreed, grinning at her new sister-in-law.

"Listen to the pot calling the kettle black," Jenni's husband injected, patting his own slightly rounded belly. "You cook as though you're serving an army, instead of just the two of us."

"Won't be just the two of you for long," Curtis said, winking. "When did you say your baby is due?"

"In a month," Jenni answered, smiling proudly. "What about you, Marcie? When is your little one due?"

Leaning her head on Ryan's shoulder, she grinned. "Three months."

"And they're going to call him Steven if he's a boy," Stevie announced.

"Rebecca if she's a girl," Becky added.

Emma rested her chin on folded hands and smiled across at Nate, seated at the other end of the long trestle table. Just that morning, when she was standing in the kitchen, her hands sticky with mushroom stuffing, he'd hugged her from behind and said, "It'll be good to have them all back again, won't it?"

And she'd sighed and said, "I've been counting the minutes."

"How long since they were all under one roof?"

"Nearly fifteen years," she said wistfully, leaning back against his strong chest.

Curtis had been the first to leave, she reminded him, having been adopted by the Joneses. Then Ryan and Stevie and Becky were taken in by the preacher and his wife. Marcie's last name changed to Henderson when the widow Henderson's son and his wife found out she didn't have any parents. Jenni, of course, had been a Wright from birth, and Judge Thompson made Matt's name change official a week after the so-called "cattle drive." The children had gone off to school, then settled in parts north and west to start their own families.

"What do you suppose ever became of Hank Campbell?" Emma had asked.

Nate kissed the back of her neck. "Last I heard, he served his time, and when he got out of prison, he married a preacher's daughter and bought a spread in Kansas."

She giggled softly. "Imagine…Hank Campbell and a pastor's daughter! Do you suppose they had any children?"

Resting his chin on her head, he'd nodded. "Twin boys and a little girl."

Emma smiled. "I'm happy for him."

That's when Nate had turned her to face him. "You're the reason he turned his life around, you know."

And when he pulled her closer, Emma said, "Nathan, my hands are a mess...you'll get egg yolk and bread crumbs all over your nice clean shirt!"

"Can't help myself," he said, touching a finger to the tip of her flour-dusted nose. "You turned my life around, too, y'know." And then he kissed her, long and hard and sweet.

Remembering the warm exchange, Emma smiled. Behind Nate, on the player piano he'd bought her for their tenth anniversary, sat the tintype rendition of their wedding day: She, standing in the grass in her flowing white gown; he, in his buttoned-up black suit sitting astride his white mare.

He remembered what she'd said that night in her parlor, about dreaming of a knight who'd come into town on a white horse and whisk her away, and rode to her house the morning after the "cattle drive," cheeks flushed and hair windblown from his ride. Dismounting, he'd dropped to one knee and took her hands in his own. "Will you be me bride, Emma Wright?"

And every day since, Emma thanked God Almighty for giving her the good sense to throw her arms around his neck and say "Yes!"

ABOUT THE AUTHOR

A prolific writer, Loree Lough has more than seventy books, sixty short stories, and 2,500 articles in print. Her stories have earned dozens of industry and Reader's Choice awards. A frequent guest speaker for writers' organizations, book clubs, private and government institutions, corporations, college and high school writing programs, and more, Loree has encouraged thousands with her comedic approach to "learned-the-hard-way" lessons about the craft and industry.

For decades, Loree has been an avid wolf enthusiast, and she dedicates a portion of her income each year to efforts that benefit the magnificent animals. She splits her time between a home in the Baltimore suburbs and a cabin in the Allegheny Mountains. She shares her life and residences with a spoiled pointer named Cash and her patient, dedicated husband, Larry, who has supported her writing and teaching endeavors throughout the years.

Loree loves hearing from her readers, so feel free to write her at loree@loreelough.com. To learn more about Loree and her books, visit her Web site at www.loreelough.com.